Suddenly a door
was flung open behind her.

An irritated male voice was saying, "Vee, I can't—"

She turned around. As she met Matt's stare, she realized how little she was wearing. She felt her face color. Deciding that dignity would make a better fig leaf, she stood her ground. She said simply, "Vee is in the kitchen."

"I thought I heard her in here. I'm sorry," Matt said. His voice had a formality, a control, that made it somehow more an acknowledgment of Eileen's half-dressed state than a wolf whistle would have been.

Eileen's heart threatened to explode through her chest wall. Time and the world stood still. Then Matt covered the distance between them in two fierce strides . . .

"Little one," he breathed, he chanted. His arms claimed her. "You're more than beautiful . . . you're desire itself. I must have you. I *will* have you!"

OUT OF A DREAM

JENNIFER ROSE

A JOVE BOOK

To WFT, who shares my dream house

The author is deeply grateful to flight attendant Irene Haber, who generously provided background information about jetliners and their crews. Any errors are, of course, the author's own.

First Jove edition published July 1981

First printing

Printed in the United States of America

Jove books are published by Jove Publications, Inc.
200 Madison Avenue, New York, N.Y. 10016

chapter 1

ALL WEEK LONG Eileen had been dreading the plane trip to Geneva.

Night after night the dark-haired gamine had raised her huge, elfin eyes heavenward and sent up childish wishes. Please let her boss change his mind and send someone else in her place. Please let her come down with the flu. Something. Anything.

Shameful wishes, she knew, when the other secretaries in the advertising agency were all turning various shades of green over Eileen Connor's glamorous assignment. Not only was she getting a paid trip to sparkling Switzerland in the middle of a dreary, slushy New York January, she was going to be working one-on-one with Alan Scott, who was the hands-down typing pool nominee for Most Gorgeous Account Executive on Madison Avenue.

But Eileen had trouble cranking up enthusiasm for Geneva, no matter how many pictures she looked at of the famous Jet d'Eau geyser spouting up out of Lake Geneva, or of handsome young couples gazing rapturously at one another over a fondue pot. The very notion of traveling—especially by plane—conjured a wealth of steamy notions she'd been doing her best to frost over.

She felt even less enthusiasm for Alan Scott. Carefully styled blond hair, insinuating blue eyes, a come-hither smile, and an all too apparent belief in his own charm didn't happen to add up to her personal definition of "gorgeous." Alan Scott, to Eileen's private thinking, looked as though he'd melt in the rain. And if he cared about anything in the world besides advertising, tennis, and keeping up his image as a womanizer, she had yet to find out what it was.

No, the idea of two weeks abroad with Alan Scott most assuredly failed to set Eileen's heart racing—except with anger and anxiety. She would much have preferred sticking to her routine of the past eight months: dizzying herself in her hectic job by day, numbing herself in thick, complicated novels by night.

Anything to keep from remembering. Anything to keep from thinking: *Keith*.

Alas, her fairy godmother had been out to lunch for a long, long time now. Eileen's wishes to be spared the trip to Geneva were resoundingly ignored.

Her boss did not change his mind about sending her on the "Swiss Mission." He kept congratulating himself, in fact, on having in his employ a secretary who spoke near-fluent French and more than a smattering of German, the two principal languages of Switzerland. He seemed to think that Eileen's destiny in life was to bring greater glory to Marsden Advertising in general, and to help Alan Scott land the Mont Blanc Watch Company account in particular.

Nor did Eileen come down with the flu. The robust health that her delicate bones and milky skin belied continued to keep the virus at bay, although half of New York was coughing.

Now Eileen was aboard Swissair flight SR 111, sitting in a window seat in an otherwise empty row, growing ever more anxious as the plane started slowly taxiing down the runway at JFK International Airport.

At least, she thought with a small sigh of relief, she would have the comfort of solitude. When she'd checked in for the flight, she'd asked the Swissair ground attendant to give her a window seat in an empty row; then she'd kept her fingers crossed that the row would stay empty. The flight was going to be hard enough without having to fight off the advances of some self-styled Romeo. She'd have ample work in that department when Alan Scott joined her in Geneva two days hence.

Flight attendants moved up and down the aisles of the jumbo jet checking that the passengers had their seatbelts fastened and their seat backs and trays upright. As Eileen looked at the relaxed, smiling hostesses in their crisp yet inviting red-accented navy and white suits, she rather repented of her own choice of traveling costume.

She was dressed all wrong for a seven-hour flight, she knew. All wrong, period. Her severe, figure-disguising gray wool dress was expensive and perfectly fashionable—if the wearer happened to be a forty-five-year-old woman with big bones. Eileen was twenty-four, size five, and getting hot under her mandarin collar. She noticed that the other young women on the flight were all wearing terrific-looking designer jeans and brightly colored shirts open at the throat. But ever since Keith had left, the great thing had been to hide: hide her body inside formidable clothes, hide her forehead under long bangs, hide her body and spirit any which way she could.

Keith, why did you do it to me? she would ask herself over and over. Why did you do it to us? Are you happier now? Do you ever think about me?

Eileen shook her head, to no avail. She couldn't disperse the unbidden, unwanted thoughts. She peered out the small window, at the rich "blue hour" tones of the early evening sky and the delicate dusting of snow on the silver wings of the plane, but she couldn't blot out the still-sharp image of Keith's face.

"Are you all right?" inquired a female voice, interrupting her reverie. "Can I get you anything?"

Eileen started and looked around. To her dismay, a stewardess was standing there looking solicitously down at her.

Mutely Eileen shook her head and prayed for the woman to go away.

"If you have some medication with you that you'd like to take, I can get you a glass of water before takeoff." The stewardess—a tall, slim, crinkly-eyed redhead whose nane tag identified her as "V. Lenke"—flashed a genuinely warm smile, not the plastic grin Eileen was steeled for.

But the smile wasn't enough to thaw Eileen. "I'm quite all right," she announced coolly. "I'm not going to be sick or anything like that."

If V. Lenke felt brushed off, she didn't show it. "I'll check on you later," she promised Eileen cheerfully and moved on down the aisle.

As the 747 taxied into position for takeoff, Eileen breathed deeply in and out. She knew what the stewardess thought—that she was afraid of flying. But she wasn't, at least not in the usual sense. Her father had been an Air Force career officer, and—like many other Air Force "brats"—she could boast that she had flown before she had walked. The thrum of the powerful Pratt & Whitney engines and the crunch of the giant wheels over the Tarmac were pleasant, almost musical sounds to her ears.

It was V. Lenke herself who was making Eileen feel like a volcano about to spew lava—V. Lenke and all the other carefully made-up, trim, easygoing hostesses.

Keith had left Eileen for an air hostess he had met on one of his many business trips around the United States. Two years of marriage had vanished into thin air, like the bright exhaust trail of a jet fading into the blue of an afternoon sky.

She wondered if he missed her, if he remembered the good times they'd had. She thought their nights were so special. Were they anything special to Keith?

A male voice came on over the loudspeaker system to give the final pre-takeoff safety instructions, and for a moment Eileen's attention was diverted. She couldn't help feeling proud of her ability to follow the steward's words in French and German as well as in English. Then the stewardesses paraded up and down the aisles pointing out emergency exits, and Eileen tasted bitterness in her mouth again.

Keith, she thought, as the jet roared into the sky.

Keith, she thought, as she glimpsed the white-capped Atlantic Ocean through a sudden clearing in the clouds.

Keith, she thought, as the NO SMOKING/DEFENSE DE FU-

MER/NICHT RAUCHEN sign went off, and the captain modified the steepness of his ascent.

Once again she was snapped back to reality by the brisk voice of V. Lenke.

"We'll be serving dinner shortly," the smiling redhead said, handing Eileen a menu card. "Would you like to purchase a cocktail first?"

Eileen had never been much of a drinker. In the good days with Keith, she'd been too high on life to want more than a glass or two of wine with dinner and an occasional light gin and tonic at a party. Then, when Keith left, she saw alcohol as a potential enemy that could make her relax her guard and get swept off her feet again, and she stayed clear of it altogether. On the few occasions she'd gone out after work with a group from the office, she'd usually ordered a Coke. Now, on impulse, she invoked the spirit of Madison Avenue and said:

"I'll have a martini, please. Extra dry."

V. Lenke's smile widened, and the lines at the corners of her eyes went deeper. Eileen grudgingly had to admit to herself that the other woman's weathery looks were somehow attractive and reassuring.

"I'm afraid our martinis are premixed," the hostess replied. "The most creative I can get is to give you an extra olive."

"Oh, that's fine," Eileen said hastily. "I don't usually— That's fine, really."

"Well, you seem to be feeling a bit better," V. Lenke announced perkily, and moved on to get other drink orders.

Eileen realized to her amazement that she was indeed feeling better—less angry, less tense. Maybe her friends back in New York had been right, after all, about the tonic effect of getting on a plane bound for an exotic destination. Or maybe staring out the window at the whooshing sky and wallowing in memories of Keith—a sweet torture she'd denied herself for months—had let some of her pain escape, like steam whistling up out of the safety valve of a pressure cooker.

And, she had to admit, V. Lenke had helped. In the eight months since her husband's abrupt departure, Eileen had developed almost a phobia about air hostesses, as though they were all the enemy, as though each one of them individually had engaged with Eileen in a tug of war for Keith's love—and had won. But it was just not possible to feel threatened by V. Lenke.

After a second martini, Eileen felt even better. She felt better yet after dinner—veal cordon bleu and a half bottle of Neuchâtel, a Swiss white wine which reminded her of a sweet, clear mountain stream, but which packed a bit more punch.

V. Lenke came along with a steaming pot of coffee. "May I refill your cup?" she asked.

"Please," Eileen said, and put her cup on the small tray the stewardess carried in her left hand. For the first time Eileen noticed the stewardess wore a gold sliver of a wedding band. The sight of that ring moved her to add, "I'm sorry if I was rude before."

"I understand," the redhead said, without a moment's hesitation. "An awful lot of passengers are edgy before takeoff." She extended the tray with Eileen's refilled coffee cup. Outside, the pitch of the engines changed slightly as the jet cruised along through the Prussian blue sky.

"Oh, it wasn't that at all," Eileen riposted. "I grew up flying. It's just—"

Suddenly, her tongue loosened by the two martinis and the wine, Eileen was pouring out the story of her marriage to Keith—and its shattering collapse when he fell in love with a stewardess.

"Well, you poor dear," V. Lenke said. "No wonder you gave me the fish eye!"

Eileen let loose a whoop of laughter, the first in ever so long, and all at once both women were giggling like teenagers.

"Look," the stewardess began, "I've got to finish coffee service, but then I'd like to come back and talk to you, if I may. We had a lot of last-minute no-shows tonight—

because of the stormy weather outside New York City—
and so the crew can take it a bit easy."

"I'd like that very much, Mrs. Lenke," Eileen agreed
warmly. "You're very easy to talk to."

"Call me Vee, for heaven's sake. My real name is Violet,
if you can believe," gesturing at her flaming hair, "but all
my friends call me Vee."

"I'm Eileen. Eileen Connor."

A few minutes later, the friendly flight attendant was
perching on the armrest of the empty aisle seat in Eileen's
row. Airline policy, she explained, frowned on hostesses
sitting in actual seats in the passenger section. Eileen moved
to the middle seat to make conversation easier.

"I suppose you really enjoy traveling," Eileen commented, with a bit of a sigh. "My family traveled so much
when I was little that what I've always wanted more than
anything was to live somewhere long enough for everyone
to know my name. And now I live in New York—and I
haven't even met the people who have apartments on either
side of me in my building!"

"I do love to travel," Vee admitted, "even after almost
twenty years of flying. Rio de Janeiro at Carnival time,
Tokyo when the cherry blossoms are in bloom—you name
the excitement, and I've been part of it. But now I have a
two-year-old baby girl—don't raise your eyebrows, Eileen,
I'm not the *only* forty-year-old in the world with a toddler—
and, to tell you the truth, I'm really happiest when I'm at
home with Pierre and little Marie."

"Where is home for you?" Eileen asked, trying to censor
the wistfulness that threatened to creep into her voice.

"Vevey. It's a small town on the other end of the Lake
from Geneva. Very pretty. Terraced hills with grapes growing everywhere— My husband is in the wine business."

"I wouldn't have guessed you were Swiss," Eileen said.
"You speak English perfectly."

"I should hope so," Vee retorted drily. "I was born and
raised in Oregon."

"Were you?" Eileen exclaimed. "We're practically

neighbors. I was born in Washington State, and that's the only place I ever came close to feeling was home—my dad was posted at McCord Air Force Base near Tacoma between stints abroad. I met Keith in Tacoma, in fact, but right after we got married he decided he wanted to head for New York. And no sooner did he uproot me and plant me on East Sixty-first Street than he went to work for a photographic supplies manufacturer who had him flying off all over the States. And that," she concluded, her voice tinged with bitterness, "was the un-greening of Eileen."

"Come on," Vee said lightly. "It was probably a good thing that you ended up in New York."

"Do you think? I like my job with the Marsden Agency, and I have a sweet little apartment—even if it's in the middle of a big, anonymous building; but I'll never totally feel at home there. Sometimes I wish—"

Her voice trailed off and Vee looked inquiringly at her. Eileen just shook her head.

"You know," Vee announced after a pause, "you need to meet a new man."

Eileen felt her face grow hot and knew her cheeks were turning scarlet. When she'd first met Keith he'd said that every time she blushed she reminded him of Snow White— jet hair, milky fair skin, and outrageously red cheeks. "The fairest of the fair," he would whisper, running proprietary fingers through her dark tangle of hair, staring into her eyes until the blush grew improbably deeper. She'd had her hair cut after he left; she'd ordered her hairdresser to tame the dark tangle to a sleek, almost forbidding, helmet. Some-times she wanted to let her hair run riot again, but the idea seemed dangerous.

Now her hand automatically went to her hair to make sure it was all in place, the armor intact.

"No," she told Vee, "I don't want to have anything to do with men at the moment. I don't need a man. I don't need anything, and I like it that way."

"Nonsense," Vee replied briskly. "You may be a bit

numb around the edges, but you're not dead yet. A divorce isn't the end of the world, you know. It could have been a lot more tragic. There could have been children involved—"

"Tell me about your daughter," Eileen interrupted, not caring how blatantly she changed the subject. "Do she and your husband mind very much when you travel?"

"Oh, I think Marie probably imagines that every mama disappears for two or three days a week. I went back to flying when she was nine months old. As for Pierre—I like to think he misses me a little, but he says my traveling gives him a chance to be with Marie that very few fathers ever have with their children. We have a housekeeper, of course, our marvelous Coco, who's there when I'm away, but there's still a very special bond between those two. At her tender age, Marie already knows that you drink *vin rouge* with some food and *vin blanc* with other food!"

The 747, which had been sailing smoothly through the sky, took a couple of bumps. The steward's voice came on over the intercom and announced that there would be a few minutes of clear-air turbulence, and would the passengers please fasten their seatbelts.

Vee Lenke stood up. "Back to work for me," she announced cheerily. "But don't think I'm letting you off the hook so easily."

"What do you mean?" Eileen wanted to know.

"Maybe I'm an interfering old busybody, but I've taken a liking to you, Eileen Connor, and I'm determined to get you out of your shell. I've got a baby brother who's getting over a bit of heartbreak himself, and something tells me the two of you ought to be thrown together. He may be in Geneva this week. He's always on the move. What do you say?"

Eileen vigorously shook her head. "I'm flattered, but—"

"'But' nothing. His name is Matt Edwards, he's an architect, he's the very definition of 'tall, dark, and handsome,' and he's the second most wonderful man in the world. And the first most impossible. Fasten your seatbelt and roll *that* around in your mind."

The stewardess made her way down the aisle checking on the other passengers, and Eileen leaned back into her seat and closed her eyes. "Matt Edwards," she repeated to herself, as the plane stuttered through the sky. To her astonishment, she felt a not-unpleasant flutter of turbulence in her heart.

chapter 2

HIGH ABOVE THE Atlantic Ocean, Eileen dreamed a recurring dream. She had somehow gotten lost deep in an echoing cave. Shadows grabbed at her; Keith's voice mocked her. And a tall, dark, ruggedly handsome man whom she knew and didn't know was reaching out to her and telling her something she desperately needed to hear, only he was telling her in French, and her French was suddenly rusty. . . .

She started awake. Reality came into focus. The commanding voice of a Swissair pilot was announcing—in a French she understood perfectly—that he was about to begin his descent into the Geneva area and expected to touch down at 7:20 A.M., precisely on schedule.

Eileen smiled at the pride in his voice. She wondered what the superpunctual Swiss would make of her—a woman who didn't own a wrist watch, who was sometimes teasingly called "the late Miss Connor." Somehow, ever since Keith's abrupt defection from their marriage, she'd found herself just a little bit out of synch with the clock. One of her coworkers at the Marsden Agency had told her that perpetual tardiness was a syndrome that signaled discontent with one's life—a theory which Eileen had waved aside as so much pop psychology. Syndrome or not, she told herself now, she'd have to try to be prompt in Geneva, especially for her appointments with the Mont Blanc Watch Company. Maybe she'd even buy one of their elegant products for herself. She had money with her for just such a special purchase.

11

Vee Lenke came hurrying down the aisle of the big jet-liner.

"Ears popping?" she cheerfully asked Eileen.

"Not yet. But a girl can hope," Eileen quipped gaily.

"It was grand chatting with you. Will you come up to Vevey some afternoon when I'm not flying?"

"I'd love to," Eileen said, with genuine enthusiasm.

"Where are you staying? I'll give you a call when I know my schedule for the next couple of weeks, and you have some idea of yours."

"Our clients suggested we stay at the Hotel Richemond. Is it nice?"

"The nicest! Right on the Lake." Vee made mischievous moves with her broad red eyebrows. "You must be sure to have a bullshot in their bar—it's a great specialty."

"Vodka and bouillon? I always thought that sounded like a ghastly drink."

To Eileen's surprise, Vee's face suddenly radiated triumph.

"Eileen Connor, did I or did I not tell you that you and my brother were made for each other? That's his opinion exactly. Look, I know you're a bit leary of this meeting, but mayn't I have him call you? So you and he can go to the Richemond Bar and *not* drink bullshots together?

For a heady moment, fragments of Eileen's dream came swirling back to her. The ruggedly handsome stranger whom she knew and didn't know: Was he Vee's brother? A vague longing tugged at her. But she shook her dark, sleek head. Matt Edwards, like Keith, was a roamer, an adventurer. And that kind of man spelled danger for her.

"I'm flattered," she told her new friend. "But I'm just not—I don't know—" She paused, searched for the precise phrase, and found it. "I'm just not in shape."

"You look in pretty good shape to me!"

Eileen smiled and looked out the airplane window at the rapidly approaching vistas of Switzerland. "Not in shape emotionally, I mean."

"Oh, I know what you mean." For a moment, the flight

attendant's animated face went somber. "I know too well.
I'm afraid Matt would say the same thing. He's still reeling
a bit from some trouble of his own; and that's yet another
reason I think you two ought to give each other a go. I
know, I know," she said as Eileen started to protest, "you're
just not going to say yes. Okay. I give up. But only for the
moment! I'll see you in Vevey. Now I better go strap myself
in, or I'm in for a lecture."

Half an hour later, Eileen was on the ground, through
customs, and staring up at the most luminous morning sky
she had ever beheld. As she got into a taxi and asked the
driver to take her to the Hotel Richemond, she began pulsing
with a sense of excitement. Suddenly she started to laugh.

"*Mademoiselle?*" the driver inquired, a bit anxiously.

"*Rien, monsieur,*" she assured him. "Nothing." How
could she explain—in French, to a stranger—that she was
laughing at herself? Half a day previously—one mere sweep
of the hands of the clock—she had been making her heavy-
hearted way to Kennedy Airport in New York. Now here
she was, exulting in the clear sky, feeling herself in the
grips of a most un-Eileen-like mystical certainty that her
life was about to change, gloriously. And there wasn't even
a tangible reason for her change of spirit.

Oh, well. She wasn't going to question herself too
deeply. What was the phrase her maternal grandmother had
uttered so often? "Happiness is its own excuse."

Her mood soared higher still as she beheld the calm,
sparkling waters of Lake Geneva, its blue rivaling that of
the sky, and the beautifully contrasting water of the River
Rhone, which fed the Lake. In the distance loomed the
snow-capped Alps, poster-perfect. Between water and
mountains rose layers of buildings, modern skyscrapers and
old stone churches. What a pleasure, she thought, to witness
such a harmonious relationship between the natural and
manmade. How different from New York, where the rivers
seemed so remote from the daily life of the city.

"Ah, yes," the cab driver answered in response to her
eager questions, "that's the Old Town across the River

Rhone. Very charming, is it not? But it is this side of the river that makes Geneva tick." He laughed at his pun about the thriving Swiss watch business, and Eileen laughed too, thrilled with her own grasp of French. "And here, *mademoiselle*," the driver said, "is your hotel."

As Eileen approached the pale façade of the Hotel Richemond, she noticed a separate entrance marked BAR. For an instant, she pictured herself having a drink there with the commanding stranger of her airborne dream, and she wondered if she'd made a mistake in refusing to allow Vee Lenke to pursue her matchmaking ambitions. Then she was inside the spacious lobby of the hotel, and her thoughts turned to the down-to-earth business of checking in.

"Good morning, *mademoiselle*," the desk clerk greeted her, in English, as if the air proclaimed her nationality and native tongue.

"*Bonjour, monsieur*," she returned in spirited French, and inquired after the rooms that had been reserved for herself and Alan Scott.

The clerk smiled, raised his eyebrows, and commented in French that *mademoiselle* spoke French without a trace of an accent. And, *certainement* there was a room ready for her immediately and one would be ready for *Monsieur* Scott when he arrived.

Eileen knew that the desk clerk was exaggerating her linguistic ability. She hadn't, after all, had much occasion to speak French in New York, though she'd tried to keep her skills current by going to French films and reading French magazines. But still she left the desk feeling pleased. Perhaps her boss had been right in insisting that Eileen Connor was cut out for big-time international assignments, like helping Alan Scott land the Mont Blanc Watch Company account. Maybe this trip would be a turning point in her career. Maybe it was time she started thinking about leaving the secretarial pool and getting into the creative end of advertising.

An elderly, courtly bellman left Eileen and her luggage

in her room. Her euphoric feelings suddenly deflated, like so many sad ballons.

The mirror.

Who was that woman in the mirror?

Was that a woman on the verge of glorious change? A darer and a dreamer?

No.

Eileen ruefully shook her head. "Oh, kid," she sighed, "come on down out of the clouds."

For the past few hours she'd looked outward, not inward, and she'd found a bit of her old pizazz, her pre-Keith lightness and strength. Now, glaring at her reflection, she was convinced that her rise in spirit, in self-esteem, was just some kind of delusion.

Okay, she conceded, the basic Eileen package wasn't bad. Her milky skin was country-fresh—or at least it would be after she washed away the streaks and stains of travel. And somewhere concealed inside her dress there was a fine, slim figure. But who would ever know it? Her suitcase was full of clothes just as unflattering as the high-necked gray wool dress she was wearing now. And the sleek helmet of hair was all wrong for her—all wrong, anyway, for the Eileen she'd once again longed to be. Oh, why couldn't Swissair have lost her luggage and given her a check to replace the contents? That would have been a start.

She sank down on the queen-size bed. She felt tears prickling behind her eyelids. She and Keith had slept in a bed just the size of this one on their honeymoon; they'd slept and they'd done some things more delicious than sleeping. . . .

She sat up straight. "Eileen Connor," she began out loud in her sternest voice, "you're being self-indulgent and silly. It's all just jet lag. Take a nap like a good girl, and then get up and shower and start making phone calls to set up appointments for Alan. That's why you're in Geneva, you know. You weren't sent here to dream about strange men and moon about your wardrobe."

She kicked off her shoes—the sensible, low-heeled shoes she'd bought perversely after the breakup because Keith had loved her in high-heeled sandals; she unzipped the now-hateful gray dress and stepped out of it; she slid between crisp sheets. But sleep wouldn't come. Even though she'd only dozed for an hour or two on the plane, she just couldn't let go of consciousness.

On sudden impulse she picked up the phone beside the bed. When the hotel operator responded, Eileen pitched her a single question: "What time do the dress shops open?"

"*Ah, c'est lundi*," the operator replied. "It's Monday." Which meant, she explained, that the big shops didn't open until noon. But if *mademoiselle* was desperate, perhaps she might like to try the boutiques in the Old Town.

Eileen thanked her and hung up. Her heart beat a little faster. Her first glimpse of the Old Town, rising steeply upward across the River Rhone, had had an oddly powerful impact on her. Something wonderful was going to happen to her there, she just knew it.

She took a long shower in the gleaming bathroom, then rubbed herself dry with a huge, thick towel. She opened her suitcase, hung up her clothes, and selected the least hopeless outfit in her wardrobe: an Italian gray knit sweater and skirt. She got out her folder of travelers' checks and did some swift calculating. She had taken several hundred dollars from her savings account because she planned to invest in a piece of important jewelry or a good watch. Clothes hardly had the same enduring value, she cautioned herself; then the born-again romantic voice she'd been hearing the last few hours said, "To hell with caution." A splurge on clothing was vastly overdue. She could go on being late a little longer.

She put on her coat, slung her purse over her shoulder, took the elevator downstairs to the lobby, and asked directions to the Old Town.

chapter 3

EILEEN WAS A woman with a purpose. She hurried across the conjunction of Lake Geneva and the River Rhone via the Mont Blanc Bridge with scarcely a glance at the fantastic four-hundred-foot-high burst of water known as the Jet d'Eau, scarcely a nod for the famous swans spangling the blue of the Lake. She was not deflected by the array of cafés on the Left Bank of the Lake—though the smell of strong coffee and fresh-baked *croissants* awoke a sudden hunger in her. She gave only a cursory courtesy glance at the famous Flower Clock, a marvel of accuracy, its twelve-foot face constructed entirely of plants that bloomed even in winter.

She would see these and other sights later. First she had to remake the woman who would do the seeing.

She turned onto the bustling rue du Rhone and then angled up the narrow, steep, winding main street of the Old Town, the Grand'rue. Instinctively, she knew she was headed in the right direction. The street itself—so very different from the broad avenues of New York—seemed to embrace her and draw her upward.

A few minutes later she knew she'd found her target. UNE VIE NOUVELLE read the sign outside a small dress shop. *A New Life*. The window was full of reds: strawberry-color skirts, magenta silk shirts, stoplight-red sweaters—all the colors of merriment and adventure, the colors of "Look at me."

Eileen pushed open the door and entered the shop. Several other early-morning browsers milled about—two very chic middle-aged blondes exclaiming over an ankle-length sweater-coat, a young student-type wistfully inquiring of a saleswoman if anything was on sale, and a man, profile facing Eileen, poring over a box of silk scarves, clearly looking for a present.

No. Not just *a* man.

The man.

The tall, dark, angular, imposing man Eileen had dreamed about on the airplane. The man in the cave who knew something she needed to know. Who maybe knew everything she needed to know.

He was even dressed similarly: rugged Irish fisherman's sweater, heavy tweed pants, hiking boots. There wafted off him the same heady aura of beautifully fused opposites: gentleness and strength, intelligence and raw jungle lusts, high consciousness and playful humorousness.

Eileen could not move. Her heart thudded to the point of pain. Her breath came raggedly. She wanted to hurl herself into the stranger's arms. She wanted to run away and hide.

Turn around, she silently begged him. Let me see your face full-on. Please, please don't be the stranger of my dreams. Disappoint me now, so you won't disappoint me later. Turn around, I implore you, and end this moment. I can't bear feeling so much. I can't bear being so naked.

As if he'd heard and wanted to obey, the man turned around. Half her prayer was answered. But only half her prayer.

No. It's not possible. He was not only the stranger from her dream, he was, she abruptly realized, the man of all her dreams. The broad planes and vital hollows of his face, the weathery skin, the totally alive dark eyes, the faintly sardonic mouth: This was scenery she could gaze on forever.

Their eyes locked. She felt her cheeks ignite, felt herself grow all the shades of red she'd seen in the window of the shop. But there wasn't any shop. Not now. No shop, no other people, no Switzerland, no world.

And then someone sneezed. One of the chic middle-aged

blondes let out a gigantic "Ah-choo," and another, and the glorious, the unbearable, moment was over. Improbably, Eileen wanted to giggle. She steadied herself and made her body pivot. Made herself start looking at dresses on a rack.

Still half-numb, she randomly plucked at hangers. She asked a saleswoman where she could try the dresses on.

A voice arrested her. His voice. Addressing her in halted, accented French that was nonetheless imperious and self-certain.

"Not those dresses," the stranger announced, the stranger commanded. "They're as bad as what you're wearing."

She looked at the dresses she was holding. For the first time, she really saw them. In her numbness, she had picked the most conservative clothes in the shop—good, dark wools of the sort that hung in her closet back at the Hotel Richemond, the very clothes she'd sought to escape.

But how could he? How dare he? She stared at him in voiceless astonishment and outrage.

"*Pardonnez-moi, mademoiselle,*" he began, with nothing at all in his voice to indicate contrition. Rather, he projected cheerfulness and casualness, as if this were a pleasant but ordinary passage in his life. "Do you understand English?" he asked her then.

"Better than you speak French," she snapped back.

She might as easily have offered him a hand to shake for all that she perturbed him. "Aha, one of my country-women," he commented. "At least I don't have to explain to you about American brashness, right?" He answered his own question with a grin.

"Look—"

"I know, I know," he interrupted. "You think I'm crazy, or maybe just insufferably rude; but I couldn't help myself. Why does a beautiful, spirited young woman hide herself in such depressing clothes? And under bangs that are all wrong for her face? You look like the young Audrey Hepburn! Or you would, if you didn't try so hard not to."

The saleswoman materialized at Eileen's elbow. "If *madame* wants to come with me, we have a dressing room free."

"No, she's changed her mind," the stranger announced breezily, in his atrocious French. He started pulling clothes off the racks. "Here," he said to Eileen, handing her a pair of crimson velvet jeans, "these'll show off your sweet little *derrière*. And what about this number?," holding up a halter-necked flame-and-pink striped sheer wool dress. "Matches your blush perfectly."

Eileen felt rooted to the floor. She was burning with anger and embarrassment. She expected the saleswoman to ask her to leave the shop. To her astonishment, the woman said instead, "*Madame* certainly has the figure and the youth for these clothes."

Ordinarily Eileen would have fled. But jet lag, lack of sleep, a faint hangover, and the spaciness that comes with being transplanted conspired to cast her into an altered state. Her anger and embarrassment dissipated. She was all at once a creature without any emotions. She felt as cool as she'd felt hot. She was indifferent. She was free.

No. Not really free. Not free of the extraordinary stranger. But free of her usual notions of herself and life: free of Eileen.

Calm and confident as a model, she went to the dressing room, slipped into the flame-and-pink dress, and walked back out to the main part of the shop.

"*Charmante!*" the saleswoman enthused. "It seems to have been made for *madame*. With your shoulders, the halter neck is perfect." She fussed around Eileen, tugging at the waist here, fastening a hook there. "Why, even the length is perfect. You could wear it right out of the shop."

"Not with those shoes, she couldn't," the stranger interjected crisply. "She needs a pair of sandals, very delicate, with a heel like this." He measured out three inches between his forefinger and thumb.

The saleswoman nodded vigorously. "Of course different shoes, *monsieur*. There is a very fine shop just around the corner from here; I will give you their card."

She handed a card to the man, and with a start Eileen realized that the woman thought he and Eileen were together. The stranger's eyes twinkled, and Eileen knew the realization had hit him simultaneously. She decided to play the moment for all it was worth.

"But darling," she pouted at the man, "you haven't said whether or not you like the dress." She pirouetted about, not minding in the least when his eyes widened with appreciation at his brief glimpse of her momentarily bared knees.

He fell into the game at once. "Haven't you known me long enough to tell when I like something? Take it. Take it. And now try on the jeans."

"I need a top to try them on with. Pick one out for me, will you, darling?"

"Try these," he was saying a moment later, handing her a white silk shirt with cerise trim, and a pale pink turtleneck sweater. He smiled and added, "Darling."

There was no question as to his opinion of the way the jeans and the sweater fit Eileen; he gave an all-American whistle. "Keep them on," he added casually, when the saleswoman walked out of earshot, "and I'll buy you breakfast. Darling."

"You are the most obnoxious man I have ever encountered," she heard herself answer, "and I would be delighted to have breakfast with you."

"Good." His matter-of-fact voice was already becoming familiar to Eileen. "Now go try on the shirt. I've got to pick out a scarf as a present for a friend—as I was earnestly doing when you so rudely interrupted me."

Eileen felt her heart go into overtime. However absurd the feeling, she was jealous—her new cool suddenly deserting her. She found herself desperately hoping that the stranger's "friend" was a plump, gray-haired, seventy-year-old librarian. But who would come to Une Vie Nouvelle to buy a present for that sort of woman?

My friend. That's how Keith had coyly referred to the airline stewardess for whom he had eventually deserted Eileen.

She retreated to the dressing room. She faced herself in

the mirror. How different she looked from the discouraging reflection she'd stared at two hours ago in her hotel room. It wasn't just that her clothes were different. Her posture was different; her color was different. Now she was looking at the Eileen she wanted to be—the old Eileen, the brand-new Eileen.

"You're gorgeous," she told her reflection. "You don't have to be jealous of anyone. You can hold your own. Don't blow everything by getting insecure. Don't give in to jealousy. Okay, kid?"

"Okay," the reflection answered; and if her voice lacked total conviction, Eileen pretended not to notice.

She gave her gray skirt and sweater to the saleswoman to pack up along with the new dress and shirt. She countersigned travelers' checks, stood patiently while the saleswoman snipped the tags from her new pink sweater and crimson jeans, and watched with what she hoped was convincing calmness as the handsome stranger paid for the scarf he'd finally chosen—a long chiffon streamer the blue of Lake Geneva.

A blonde, Eileen thought. That scarf is for a blue-eyed blonde. Then he turned a gaze of undisguised admiration her way, and her panic eased.

"Let's go to the Clemence," he said.

"What's that?"

"The most popular café in the Old Town. I want to show you off." He guided her out of the shop. "Don't you know Geneva at all? No. Wait," as she started to answer. "Don't tell me. Not yet. I don't want to know if you just got to Geneva or if you've lived here all your life. I don't want to know anything about you. Not your facts, I mean. If you're married and the mother of five, I don't want to know. If you're a student who's about to catch the train back to Paris and disappear forever, I don't want to know. And I don't want you to know about me. Not my details. Later, yes. Everything later."

He came to a dead halt. He put strong hands on her shoulders. Fantastic currents sizzled up and down her arms.

"I've never had an encounter quite like this one," he said. His clear, sure voice was husky now. "I'm terrified it's a dream I'm going to wake up from. Tell me you feel something special, too. Tell me we're not going to crash."

Pedestrians detoured around them. A motorcyclist came roaring by, yelled something Eileen couldn't catch, and zoomed on up the hill. As Eileen spoke, she had the sensation that her words were coming from far away, from some source other than her own head. The stranger, the motorcyclist, the pedestrians, and she were all characters in a play. The words she was speaking were part of a script.

"You know I'm feeling what you're feeling," she said. "You don't want to hear my story because you already know everything about me that matters. I've never met another man like you. You know that too."

He looked at her. His grip tightened until her arms ached, but she didn't flinch. He looked at her with such urgency that her lips felt kissed, her breasts felt caressed.

"My God," he murmured, "I'm dying to get my hands on your hair and push it back off your face. You ought to wear it in a wild tangle, you know. Or a street-urchin cut. Not that dreary bob."

She felt a sudden burst of fury. "Who are you? Pygmalion?" she asked heatedly. "Is this the first act of *My Fair Lady*? Are you making me over for a *Cosmopolitan* magazine article?"

His hands fell away from her arms. "Ah, crashing so quickly," he said sadly. Then he laughed, pure merry peals of laughter, childlike innocent laughter devoid of all sting. "Proud little creature, aren't you?" he said. "Proud and sensitive. That's a tricky combination, you know. Do you hate me beyond redemption now? Or will you still permit me the honor of buying you breakfast?"

In spite of herself, Eileen started laughing too. The script simply demanded laughter.

Passers-by stared, but she didn't care. The laughter was as curative and refreshing as some magic mineral water.

Her fury vanished as quickly as it had arisen. Whoever

this man was, it was impossible not to get mad at him—and equally impossible to stay mad at him.

Naturally as anything, she linked arms with him as they continued up the twisting cobblestone incline of the Grand'rue. "I have to admit I'm desperate for coffee," she told her intriguing companion. "If that isn't telling you more about me than you can bear to know."

"*Touché*, my little one. Do you mind terribly if I address you as 'little one'?"

"Be my guest. If you don't mind my addressing you as 'tall stranger.'"

"It sounds like a movie, doesn't it?" he said. "*Little One and the Tall Stranger*. I can see it on marquees everywhere. Starring the young Audrey Hepburn and—?"

She reran some old favorite films in her mind, then she knew. "The young Gary Cooper. Of *The Fountainhead*. Or *High Noon*."

"I can live with that."

They continued on up the hill in companionable silence. Now and then Eileen heard a faint buzzing in her head, a beating of butterfly wings; then the buzzing would go away and she would feel that she had always been in this place, with this man.

They came to a large, open, asymmetrical space where many roads converged. A bell tolled ten o'clock. Eileen looked up and realized they were standing in the shadow of a cathedral. Houses, shops, and cafés abounded. The space—he said it was called the Place de Bourg-de-Four—was almost a miniature village.

"That's the Clemence," the tall stranger said, pointing to one café. "Hangout of students, U.N. diplomats, moviemakers, university professors, journalists, tourists, and others. Shall we?"

They sat down at a small corner table. The stranger ordered *café au lait*—coffee mixed half and half with steamed milk—and *croissants* for them both. They quickly drained their cups and devoured the small, flaky, crescent-shaped rolls. The stranger ordered another round.

Eileen heard French, Italian, English, German, what she was pretty sure was Russian, and several languages she could not identify. She saw ragged jeans, the latest in French *haute couture*, Arab headdresses, and an African *dashiki*.

Mostly she heard the voice of the tall stranger—that maddeningly self-assured voice, faintly gravelly, with the sound of an ironic smile built in; mostly she saw the tall stranger's angular face, and the way a shock of dark hair continually threatened his forehead, and the way his hands sliced the air when he was making a point.

Never before, she thought. Never again. I am lost. I am found.

Their conversation was deliberately impersonal. Yet, as they discussed movies they'd enjoyed, international politics, food, sports, and the various characters they spotted at the Clemence, Eileen felt she was revealing more of herself—and learning more about the stranger—than she would have if they'd swapped life stories.

"We argue well," he commented in his offhand way, after they'd aired opposing views on the exploration of outer space. (He was all for it. She thought the money should be used to fight poverty on earth.) "I have a feeling we'd do a lot of things well. Ah, that blush becomes you madly, little one." He sandwiched one of her hands between both of his. "I have a business appointment. And you look as though you didn't sleep last night—please don't tell me why—and you want to go home and nap all day. Will you have dinner with me tonight? I have to see you in that new dress."

Eileen's throat went dry. She could not meet his gaze; then she met it. Slowly she shook her head. "I'm afraid. No, not what you think. I'm afraid—" She drew a deep breath. "We'll only let each other down. Let's just walk away from each other. That way we'll always have this morning to hold on to."

"You're a romantic, little one. I am too. But I'm afraid that won't work. Not for me, at least. I want more. And if tonight it suddenly turns out that we have nothing more to say to each other, I think, by God, that I'll be relieved. I didn't mean to fall in love again."

"Please," she murmured. "Don't use words like that. Don't tell me anything you don't mean. Promise me. Please."

"Tell me you'll have dinner with me, and I'll promise you anything."

"I'll have dinner with you," she said. "Now promise."

"I will never tell you anything I don't mean, criss-cross my heart and hope to die, stick a needle in my eye. Is that good enough?"

She smiled at the child's litany. "Good enough."

"Oh, incidentally, that holds for what I've already said, as well. Only truth has sprung from these lips, little one, since you first crossed my path. Where shall we have dinner? Back here in the Old Town?"

"That would be lovely."

"Do you remember a place we passed on the Grand'rue coming up here? The Chandelier? Or were you too much in love to see?"

"I remember," smiling again.

"The Chandelier at eight, then. You'll really come?"

"You'll really be there?" Eileen returned.

The tall stranger signaled for his check. Then he said to Eileen, "Do you see that rather grumpy looking woman across the room? The one in the brown tweed suit?"

"Yes."

"Do you know why she's frowning with such vast disapproval?"

"I haven't the faintest idea," Eileen said.

"Because she thinks I'm going to kiss you. And people don't do that sort of thing in the cafés of Geneva."

Again Eileen's heart thudded and her mouth went desert-dry. "Don't they?"

"Not very often. But now and then. Under exceptional circumstances."

He gripped her arms. So much feeling coursed through her body that she felt in danger of fainting. She was a shimmering star in a distant sky. A gigantic white-capped wave about to crest.

His lips found hers. Lingered. Pressed home. Withdrew.

The star exploded across the sky. The wave crested, crashed, and was swept out to sea.

chapter 4

EILEEN ABRUPTLY CAME to in a darkened room. Where am I? she wondered, with a rising sense of panic. What time is it? Am I late? Where am I supposed to be? Did I lose something? Why do I feel so strange?

As her eyes grew accustomed to the dimness, answers started falling into place, and with the answers a measure of calmness.

She was in her room at the Hotel Richemond, draperies drawn against the afternoon sun. It was a few minutes past four, according to the battered old traveling alarm clock on her bedside table. She wasn't late for anything. She was sure she wasn't late. And what she'd lost was—

She sat up, turned on the light, and looked in the mirror opposite.

Hair was what she'd lost. The sleek helmet was gone. Her dark locks had been chopped into a jagged urchin do.

Her fingers explored the feathery layers. They liked what they felt. As for the way she looked: Why, she looked rather like the young Audrey Hepburn.

"Oh!" she gasped aloud. More details came tumbling into her consciousness. Meeting the tall stranger, and going to the Café Clemence with him, and kissing him, and leaving him, and buying high-heeled red leather sandals, and having her hair cut, and falling exhausted into her bed . . .

The kiss. Her mind hop-scotched back to the kiss. Her lips seemed to swell with the memory of it. Her stomach ached sweetly.

Then panic rode into her mind again, wearing a long blue chiffon scarf. Who was the friend that scarf was for? Who was the stranger himself? Another heartbreaker like her ex-husband, Keith? A practiced womanizer like Alan Scott? She glanced at her clock again. In a little under four hours she would know. Maybe.

Meanwhile, she reminded herself, she had work to do. A lot of work. She was still a secretary at the Marsden Agency, not just a heroine in a romantic drama. Alan Scott would be arriving the following afternoon after a hectic day and a half in London, and he'd expect to find a full agenda on his desk.

Eileen yawned. Bed felt delicious. She'd always loved hotel beds with their crisp, taut sheets. So tempting just to slide under again. To give herself over to thoughts of the stranger.

Her stomach ached again, not so sweetly. Four hours until their meeting at the Chandelier: Could she endure that long without a glimpse of him? And what if—oh, damn the unbearable thought—what if he didn't appear? What if their adventure that morning had been a lark, a game for him? She buried her face in the pillow in a useless effort to blot out the awful scenario that came to her mind: the tall stranger, sardonic grin on his face, having dinner that night with a worldly blonde swathed in a blue chiffon scarf, her face aglow with amusement as he recounted his hour of playing Pygmalion with a deluded little American girl.

No, she told herself emphatically. I kissed him. I tasted him. He's not like that. He really wants me. He'll be there.

The telephone on her bedside table jangled. *It's the stranger*! Eileen thought with an irrational surge of hope. He can't wait four hours either. But of course he didn't know her name or where she was staying. Heart pounding wildly nonetheless, she reached for the phone.

"Hello?"

"London calling Miss Eileen Connor," an operator said.

"This is Eileen Connor."

Then Alan Scott was on the line. "Hi, baby."

"Hello, Alan," she said, wishing as usual that she could cure him of his promiscuous use of endearments.

"How are things in the land of cheese and chocolate?"

"It's beautiful here. I think you'll like the hotel. High ceilings, pale carpets—very grand."

"Never mind the carpets. Any hotel that's housing Eileen Connor would look good to me."

Eileen forced herself to count to three, slowly. Then she asked how his business in London was going.

"Business?" he countered. "Oh yeah, I also came here for business. I wish you could have seen me on the tennis court this morning. One of London's poshest indoor clubs. I was a sensation."

"I'm sure," she said sweetly, "that you've been scoring well all over London."

"Point, game, and match to Eileen Connor. Look, baby, could you line up some court time for me in Geneva? Maybe the Mont Blanc people have entrée to one of the good clubs. Tell 'em I'll be happy to reciprocate when they're in New York."

"What about a partner?"

"Sweetie, Alan Scott doesn't have trouble finding partners. If someone at Mont Blanc wants to play, fine. Otherwise, I'm sure I'll manage. You really should have seen the way I was serving today. Pow. I served two aces, what do you think of that?"

"That's wonderful, Alan. Did you get the account?"

"You are a conscientious creature, baby. Of course I did. We've got Freddie Taylor's Airways signed on the dotted line. They want to blitz America—print ads, TV, the works. Pretty good, eh what? We'll give what's-his-name a run for his money."

Her enthusiasm was real this time. "Terrific! I just hope things go as well here. Speaking of which, I'd better get down to work."

The connection went fuzzy for a moment, then Alan was saying, "You mean you haven't been working? What *have* you been doing? Don't tell me you started without me, baby. I knew I should have flown over with you. You know what they say about quiet girls—and they're right!"

"I've really got to go now, Alan. See you tomorrow. Have a good flight."

"How could winging toward you be anything but super? Cheerio. Save some for me."

It was a good thing, Eileen thought as she hung up, that Alan hadn't known she was in bed while she was talking with him. His quips would have been utterly unbearable. Oh, well. At least he'd managed to get her mind off the tall stranger and back onto the advertising business.

She got up, smoothed over the bed so it wouldn't lure her, called room service and ordered a big pot of coffee, splashed cold water on her face, and drew a plaid flannel robe around her fair, slim body. She took a notepad and blue felt-tip pen from her suitcase and put them on the bedside table.

A knock sounded at the door. Could it be room service already? Swiss hotels were famous for their efficiency, but this was spectacular speed.

It wasn't room service. It was a bellman, holding a rather lush and utterly Swiss arrangement of hothouse flowers— yellow roses, daisies, blue irises, flesh-color tulips, and fiery freesia springing up out of a ceramic fondue pot.

Again she irrationally thought: *The stranger*!

"*Mademoiselle* Connor?" the bellman inquired. "I'm so sorry. These were supposed to be in your room when you arrived. But they were by mistake put in the room reserved for your colleague. Where would you like them?"

"On the dresser, please." She went to her purse and found a two-franc piece for a tip. Trembling, she looked at the card. "*Bienvenue à Genève*," it said. "Welcome to Geneva." It was signed by Jean-Claude Longemalle, president of the Mont Blanc Watch Company.

So! The head of one of the landmark Swiss corporations bothered to send flowers to a secretary. Was this Old World courtesy—or a clever bit of business strategem? Whatever, the flowers certainly made a gorgeous splash against the ivories and beiges of her room.

She looked into the mirror. A bright-cheeked creature with vibrant short hair looked back at her. "Well, kid," she addressed her reflection, "no one can say your life is dull. A tall stranger taking you to breakfast, a flirtatious call from London, beautiful posies from the head of a major Swiss corporation: not bad for an old winter Monday!" Suddenly she wished Keith could know about this day—Keith who probably believed that her every waking hour was spent in man-less solitude, missing him. "Not any more, my dear," she murmured, hoping he picked up vibrations from the thought.

Then her coffee was there, rich and steaming hot, and her mind turned to business. She picked up the telephone and got the Mont Blanc people on the line. Within fifteen minutes she had meetings lined up with the advertising director, the vice-president in charge of their new American sales campaign, and Jean-Claude Longemalle himself; she'd accepted an invitation to tour the actual watch factory; and she'd even managed to secure a visitor's card to Le Club Tennis for Alan. She then called the club and reserved a court for the following evening at eight. She had a feeling that it would be to her advantage to have Alan tired at night.

Her clock said five-forty-five. She went to her windows and pulled back the draperies. Across the River Rhone, the Old Town was lighting up. Down on the Lake, a small sailboat was coming home to its dock. Suddenly she felt a prickling of tears, a rawness in her throat. This was the hour of the day when she felt most vulnerable. She wanted to be the woman some man came home to every evening at this time. She wanted to be a dock, she wanted to be the light that got lit at dusk. No day of adventures and compliments, however heady, could change that fundamental fact.

Where was the tall stranger now? Was he looking out

a window thinking thoughts like hers? Hard to believe. He had a perpetually restless look about him. He might like the idea of some little woman keeping the home fires burning, but would he want to be there with her, night after night? Or would she be the safe harbor he would sail into now and then when the seas got lonely and stormy?

That's what Keith would have liked. If he'd had his way, he would have kept Eileen and had his stewardess "friend" as well. And maybe other friends, too. "If a marriage is basically good," he liked to say, "what difference does it make what you do on the side? If anything, playing around gives the marriage spice."

But that wasn't how Eileen saw marriage. Her parents had a great monogamous romance and that was what she wanted for herself. Besides, she had to admit now that she was at a safe remove, her marriage with Keith hadn't been all that great at the core. Their values were so different.

Funny that it had been sex that finally split them. Sex had been the glue of the marriage. Though in a way it had also been their weakness—the connection they fell back on when the conversation faltered or a fight loomed just around the corner.

She drew the draperies on the vista and her thoughts. It was time to start getting ready for her date. She had made up her mind to pamper herself with the sort of beauty ritual she hadn't indulged in since Keith. Long perfumed bath, manicure, pedicure, careful makeup job to enhance her newly bared face: the works. She needed a good hour and a half. And the stranger had told her not to be late.

At seven-thirty she once again faced her full-length mirror. "Not bad, old girl," she murmured. She had to admit that the stranger had been right all around. The brief, wispy haircut, the red halter-necked dress, and the high strappy sandals conspired to make her look both bold and fragile. She seemed a woman of the world and a tomboy. She was too honest not to realize that heads would probably turn when she walked into the Chandelier.

The stranger deserved no less. Her heart pulsed furiously as her mind remembered their kiss and rehearsed for a replay. Then she headed downstairs.

"Taxi, *madame*?" the doorman inquired.

She thanked him and shook her head. She was in good time. She would walk across the Mont Blanc bridge, turn right on the rue du Rhone, and angle up the Grand'rue. A few licks of breeze off the Lake would only enhance the careful carelessness of her new hairstyle.

She traced the route she'd taken that morning; at least she thought she was tracing it. But something felt wrong. The park she was walking by was very lovely, only she didn't remember a park. She fumbled in her bag for her guidebook. It wasn't there. It was still in the larger purse she'd carried by day.

She hailed the first person she passed. He replied in German that he didn't speak French, and Eileen was so thrown that for the moment she forgot that she spoke German. She heard the cathedral bells strike eight. Her heart sank. She should be right near the cathedral, and the bells sounded alarmingly remote.

Finally a young couple helped her out. She'd overshot the Grand'rue; she was close to the University. The quickest way to the Chandelier would be up the rue St. Leger to the Bourg-de-Four, where she'd had breakfast with the stranger, then down the rue de l'Hotel de Ville, which turned into the Grand'rue.

She repeated the directions, got two nods of confirmation, and hurried off as quickly as her new high-heeled sandals would permit. She passed a café and thought of ducking inside and trying to telephone the Chandelier. But how could she explain that she wanted to speak with someone whose name she didn't know? It would take less time to walk, even in—*blast them*—those sandals.

The twists and turns of the cobblestone streets started to look familiar. Finally she had her bearings. She heard the quarter-hour strike, and moments later she was at the Chandelier.

She was at the Chandelier. The tall stranger was not.

Not at the little sit-down bar where their rendezvous was supposed to happen; not in the dining room.

Her stomach churned. She made herself sit down and order a glass of white wine. Maybe he was late himself. Maybe he was in the men's room. Maybe he'd given up on her ever arriving.

No, she told herself fifteen dreadful minutes later, the answer was plain and simple. He'd never come at all. He'd never intended to come. The greatest adventure of her life was some miserable sadist's idea of a clever joke.

"*Mademoiselle*?" a deep voice inquired in her ear.

She whirled around on her barstool. The man addressing her was a kind of Continental Alan Scott—slick dark hair, sleek suit with wide lapels and nipped-in waist, and lots of leer in his smile. Could he have the pleasure of buying *mademoiselle* another glass of wine, he wanted to know.

She thanked him with bare civility and said no. Funny, she thought to herself, a lot of the women she worked with would probably think he was devastatingly attractive, more attractive than the tall stranger. But he left her utterly cold.

Everything left her utterly cold just now.

She paid for her wine and headed down the Grand'rue toward her solitary rented bed.

chapter 5

Forget him. Forget him. Forget him.

Eileen's blue felt-tip pen traced the same message over and over on Tuesday morning, as if engaged in automatic writing. To no avail. No matter how many times she wrote the words, no matter how many times she read them, the agony of the stranger's absence from the Chandelier still owned her mind and mood.

She put the flamboyant red dress in the back of her closet and stuffed the crimson velvet jeans into a drawer. These were mere gestures, as she knew well. She had only to catch a reflection of her cropped dark hair to remember the stranger's dark hair, and his all-knowing eyes, and his faintly sardonic mouth, and his hands on her shoulders, his lips on her lips—*oh, damn him!*

She managed to lose herself for an hour by going over the presentation she and Alan Scott would be making to the people at the Mont Blanc Watch Company. The best art director and copywriter at the Marsden Agency had worked on the presentation for weeks. There were dummy ads for quality magazines like *The New Yorker*; proposed TV spots; suggestions for billboards; and an overall game plan complete with detailed budget.

"When you've reached the peak, you're ready for a Mont Blanc watch." That was the theme of the campaign. Photographs of the famous snow-capped mountain figured heavily in the ads. Eileen crossed her fingers and hoped that Jean-Claude Longemalle and the others at Mont Blanc would go for it.

The telephone rang and shattered her serenity. She cursed her pounding heart. Will I never again hear a phone, she thought, without wondering if it's him?

The caller was Vee Lenke. At the sound of her new friend's warm and eager voice, Eileen almost broke. It would feel so good to pour out the whole incredible story of her folly. But pride held her back. When Vee asked her how she was enjoying Geneva, Eileen extolled the breath-taking views and the luxuriousness of her hotel.

"Will you come out to Vevey and see us this weekend?" the stewardess asked. "I'm flying tomorrow and Thursday, and then I'm off until the following Monday. If you think the Lake is beautiful from there, you should see it from here."

"I'd like to do that," Eileen answered, though at the moment she didn't want to do anything but crawl under the bed.

Vee hesitated then asked, "Would you mind awfully if my brother Matt is here? I know you don't want to be fixed up with him, but he popped into town on business, and he'll be staying with us this weekend."

"Oh, Vee, you're terrible."

"I am, aren't I? But at least I'm telling you instead of just springing him on you. It won't be awkward like a date—just a friendly family romp."

Eileen sighed. The last thing on earth she needed was to meet another man now. Not that he would be anything but a pale ghost of the stranger. Not that any man ever would.

Vee's voice cut into her thoughts. "To tell you the ab-solute truth, Eileen, I'm not sure he's even available at the moment. He's not saying anything just yet, but he's got that look he always has when he's fallen for someone new. Another disaster, I don't doubt. He has a genius for finding Ms. Wrong."

"Are you just trying to challenge me?" Eileen teased, though she was pretty sure Vee was too straight-arrow to do anything of the sort.

"Criss-cross my heart and hope to die, stick a needle in my eye," Vee said; and if she heard Eileen gasp at the phrase she attributed the sound to static on the line. "I'm absolutely on the level. Do come meet my husband and my baby. And come meet Matt as a friend. Friendship is something he's better at than romance."

Eileen capitulated. She just couldn't bear to be rude to Vee. And she had a feeling that it might be convenient to have weekend plans that put some distance between her and Alan Scott. They set a date for Saturday noon. Vee said she could drive in to Geneva to pick up Eileen, or Eileen could take the train that wound its way along the Lake. Eileen said she rather liked the sound of the train.

"We'll have fun, I guarantee," Vee said. She hesitated for a moment and then added, "Are you sure everything is okay, Eileen?"

"Everything's fine, really."

"I thought your voice—oh, never mind. Pierre says I cluck over people too much. It's probably the connection. The better the weather the worse the phone connections here, isn't it odd? I do hope this weather holds for you. Are you doing something wonderful today?"

"The man I work with is due in this afternoon. This morning—" She bit her lip. *This morning I'm going to get back into bed and cry*, she almost said. But why worry good-hearted Vee? "This morning I'm going to see some sights," she quickly ad-libbed. "Maybe I'll go to the Palace of Nations. Or one of the museums."

"You must be sure and go to the Old Town," Vee instructed. "I never can understand why, but some visitors never get there. Splendid architecture. Matt's the one who really made me appreciate it—he's an architect, you know."

"I remember," Eileen said. She managed to add, "I went to the Old Town yesterday, actually." She swallowed hard. "I better go now," she finished quickly, before Vee could inadvertantly rub any more salt in her wounds. "I'm looking forward to Saturday."

She was trembling, actually trembling, when she hung

up the phone. Her stomach was doing flip-flops. "This won't do, kid," she muttered. She went into the bathroom and splashed cold water on her face, then repaired her makeup. She decided to redeem her lie to Vee and to go to the Palace of Nations. Not only was the building itself— the largest in Europe—supposed to be spectacular, it afforded what her guidebook said was the best view of the summit of Mont Blanc. She thought that the people at the Mont Blanc Watch Company might be pleased that she'd gone to the trouble to see the famous mountain for which they'd named their product.

The day was genuinely made for sightseeing, she had to admit to herself when she got outside. There was a January snap to the air, but no real bite. The breeze coming in off the Lake was offset by a remarkably strong sun. The few white clouds in the sky were almost needed to buffer the brilliance of the blue in which they floated serenely.

She turned her back on the Lake—and on the wrenching sight of the rising slope of the Old Town—and went to catch the bus for the Palace of Nations. An American tourist, male, middle-aged, probably married, sat down next to her for the brief ride and did his best to strike up conversation. He didn't even succeed in making her feel flattered. At the moment she could have happily done without the whole male half of the human race.

The massive white simplicity of the Palace of Nations lifted Eileen's spirit. She watched an international array of men and women hurrying up and down the broad steps leading to the building, and she almost felt the dedication wafting off them. She delivered a little lecture to herself. Think of the concerns on their minds, she told herself. Having to battle against hunger and ignorance, trying to stave off war. How can you brood about your own little disappointment in the face of all that?

But a hurt heart does not always listen to reason. A moment later she glimpsed a dark head of hair and a lean, tall body in clothes like the clothes the stranger had been wearing, and her spirit plummeted again. She went to the spot her guidebook suggested for an optimum view of Mont Blanc, and the thought foremost in her mind was that seeing the mountain with *him* would have been a hundred times as delicious.

She decided to walk the mile or so back to the hotel instead of taking the bus. The sweet, cold air soon revved up her appetite and reminded her that she'd skipped breakfast. She picked a restaurant at random and ordered a Swiss specialty, air-dried beef sliced so thin that it was transparent, and served with the tart, crunchy little pickles known as *cornichons*.

And the thought foremost in her mind was that eating *viande des Grissons* with *him* would have been a thousand times as delicious.

In a curious way she was almost relieved when Alan Scott knocked on her door that afternoon. It wasn't that he'd grown any less irritating. It was that the very nature of his personality was such a handful, a mindful, that there was no room for thoughts of the stranger.

"Bay-bee!" was the first word out of his mouth. "That's some sensational haircut! I always knew you were a looker, but I never knew you were a double for Audrey Hepburn." Then, as Eileen winced, "Did I say something wrong? That was my idea of a very big compliment. You should have done it years ago, baby. Well, aren't you going to invite me in?"

Eileen stepped aside and steeled herself for the inevitable next words.

"That's some big bed you have, baby. Me, they gave twin beds. Not what you'd call skimpy, but *this*—" He paused for effect. "This isn't a bed, it's a playground."

"Well, I left my pail and shovel back in New York," Eileen answered crisply. "What do you say we get down to business?" She moved across the room to a leather-topped maple desk.

They went over the presentation. Alan was a master of the direct-eye gaze, the pithy phrase, and Eileen had to admit that he was very charming and convincing—at least when he talked about "the marketplace" and "demographic studies." She listened to him practice his pitch and she grew steadily more certain that the people at Mont Blanc would be impressed. She told him so.

Alan's face took on an air it seldom wore—one of somberness. "I hope you're right, baby," he said. "But they've gotten along without selling in America so far, and they may still be wary about making the investment. Nobody has money to throw away these days, not even the most successful watch company in Geneva. After all, they have pretty good sales to Americans traveling here. They may not think it's worth the risk to invest in a big ad campaign just to get another small piece of the market."

"But if money is tightening up," Eileen pointed out, "maybe fewer Americans will be coming to Switzerland."

"People who have to worry about the price of an air ticket can't afford a Mont Blanc watch anyway."

Eileen looked at one of the dummy ads spread out on the desk. "This says 'Mont Blanc watches are now available at Saks Fifth Avenue and other fine department stores.' Aren't all the arrangements already made?"

"Tentative arrangements, baby. That's the name of this game. We don't have this deal locked up by any means. We've got to sell, sell, sell." He cast a cold eye on her chocolate tweed suit. "Hey, don't take this wrong, but do you have anything a little—shall we say—zippier to wear for the first meeting with Longemalle and crew? Something to show off the fabulous figure I suspect you have?"

Eileen flushed angrily. "I believe I was sent over with you because I speak French and German," she rapped out, "not because of my appearance."

"I didn't mean to offend your feminist sensibilities." Alan grinned. "I just happen to know that old man Longemalle has an eye for the ladies. So any glamour you projected would not go wasted."

Inadvertently Eileen's eyes glanced over to the vibrant arrangement of flowers Jean-Claude Longemalle had sent. The tulips had opened. With their flesh-color petals, they looked like hungry mouths. She felt oddly disturbed. *Men! Oh, men!*

Alan's eyes traced the path hers had taken. "Longe-malle?" he guessed correctly.

"Yes."

"Aha! I figured they were from some new admirer you met on the plane, but I decided to be discreet and not ask questions."

"Alan Scott, you are incapable of discretion. I bet you just didn't notice them. You're not the sort of man who sees flowers. I bet you haven't really looked at the view, either."

His pale eyes twinkled. He bowed his blond head in mock shame. He went to the window and stared out. "Beautiful. Is that Mont Blanc over there?"

"Oh, you're hopeless. Does it look anything like Mont Blanc? No, that's Le Salève. You can walk up it in three hours, my guidebook says."

"*You* can. That's not my idea of a good time. How come I don't see Mont Blanc? I thought it was the tallest mountain in Switzerland."

Eileen groaned. "It's in France, didn't you know that? And it's the tallest mountain in *Europe*. But it's fifty miles away. You have to go over to the Palace of Nations to get it in your sight lines. You better get all that straight before we have our meetings tomorrow. It's probably a lot more important than what I wear," she added tartly.

"You're right," he admitted humbly. "I don't want to come on sounding like the Ugly American. What do you say we have dinner together tonight and you clue me in?"

"I can lend you my guidebook. That will tell you everything you need to know. Besides, I've booked you a court for eight o'clock at Le Club Tennis."

"Cancel the court. I'd rather have dinner with you."

"I'm tired," Eileen said. "I want to be fresh tomorrow. I think I just want to go to bed."

"Bed sounds fine with me," Alan shot back. Then, seeing her expression of distaste, he grabbed her hand. "I'm sorry, Eileen," he said with genuine contriteness. "I know the *Playboy* patter turns you off. I really like you as a person and I respect your brains and I need to know about Mont Blanc and all of that, and if you'll have dinner with me tonight I promise, I absolutely promise, to behave like a Boy Scout."

He looked at her with such puppy eagerness that Eileen couldn't help thawing a little. Besides, she owed her smashing new red dress a genuine debut in the world.

But would he really behave himself? And even if he did, wouldn't she spend the evening mentally comparing him with the stranger—and dying inside?

"Please," he said. "You can even bring your mother, if you like."

She couldn't help smiling. And, with a sudden flash of insight, she realized he was probably feeling lonely, and nervous about the presentation to Longemalle. Even though he'd scored a success in London, he might find himself in a shaky position at the Marsden Agency if he returned to New York without the Mont Blanc Watch Company signed to a deal.

"Okay," she agreed. "Do you want me to make a reservation somewhere?"

"You're not my secretary tonight, you're my guest. And my colleague and tour guide and pal. All right with you? I'll pick a place and make a reservation—if I can borrow your guidebook. Seven-thirty sound okay?"

She handed him the guidebook. "Seven-thirty sounds terrific. Now go away and let me nap, or I'll fall asleep in my bath and drown, and who'll do your interpreting tomorrow?"

"Who indeed?" He kissed her briefly and chastely on the cheek. And added, as he was leaving, "You're a very good kid, Eileen Connor."

Several hours later Alan Scott was saying, "You're a terrible woman, Eileen Connor. You get me to promise to be on my best behavior, and then you wear a dress that would tempt a saint."

Eileen laughed. She'd had a brief nap and a long bath.

She was all set to have a pleasant, if not earth-shaking, evening. Alan Scott, she'd decided, was basically an okay person. Maybe they really could be colleagues and pals.

She gathered up her coat and purse. "You look pretty sharp yourself." He was wearing a dark pin-striped suit that accentuated his narrow waist, a gleaming white shirt with French cuffs bound together by flamboyant jade cufflinks, and a multicolor Emilio Pucci tie. He was too citified and too soft-looking—despite the tennis—to set her heart racing, but she was beginning to appreciate why he turned other women on.

"Why don't you just carry your coat?" he suggested. "I thought we'd start out right here at the Richemond with a drink at the bar, since your guidebook proclaims its virtues. Then I thought we could go to a place called Le Chat d'Or and have fondue—and a good look at the Lake."

"I read about Le Chat d'Or. That's a wonderful plan."

"What does Le Chat d'Or mean, anyway?" Alan asked, as they headed for the elevator.

"The Golden Cat."

"Ugh. I hope that's not what they're serving tonight."

"No fear," Eileen teased. "The Swiss respect gold much too much to eat it."

They crossed the lobby and walked through a revolving door into the famous Richemond Bar.

"If a mere pal is permitted to say so," Alan murmured, "I'm very proud to be walking in here with you. Do you want to sit at the bar or at a— Eileen! Are you all right?"

She clutched his arm. "Am I all right?" she repeated inanely, great pauses between each word.

"Eileen, what's the matter?" His voice went high with anxiety. "I've never seen anyone lose color so quickly. Your hands are as cold as ice. Do you want to go back upstairs?"

"I want to sit down. At a table. That table. Right there. Right there," she repeated in French, as the headwaiter greeted them.

Yes, that table was perfect. It would afford her a full-face view of a man at another table who was staring, glaring at her with terrible eyes.

Not just *a* man. *The* man.

Her tall stranger. Who was sharing his table with a worldly-looking blonde, her swan neck swathed in a blue chiffon scarf.

chapter 6

EILEEN ORDERED A MARTINI. Alan raised his eyebrows.

"Since when?" he asked. "The last time I saw you with the martini crowd, you were drinking Coke."

"Oh, things change," she replied obscurely. She could not take her eyes off the stranger, who could not take his off her. Alan and the stranger's companion were simply taking up space on the stage, two supporting players with their backs to the action, two pretty props, totally unaware.

Why is he looking at me that way—with such contempt? Doesn't he feel any shame? Eileen wondered. Has he told that woman about the joke he played on me? Oh God, I'd like to do something awful to him, she cried to herself. I'd like to make him suffer the way he made me suffer, is making me suffer still.

Eileen's martini arrived, in a fine thin crystal version of the classic martini glass; and with it the bullshot Alan had asked for out of fealty to the guidebook. He raised his drink and pronounced: "To my new pal. Long may she wave." He took a sip to seal the toast.

"To my favorite Boy Scout," she returned, and gravely touched her glass to his. The stranger, a few yards away, near enough to see her gestures, too far too hear her soft words, seemed to flinch. Inwardly she rejoiced.

I know his type, the rotter, she thought bitterly. He'd like to think I'm hung up on him. Still too crushed by his standing me up last night to look at another man. Just like Keith.

She smiled brilliantly at Alan. He returned the smile with a look of concern.

"Hey, baby, forgive my asking, but you don't take *pills* or anything, do you?" He put a casual hand on top of one of her hands. "I've just never seen anyone go through such lightning changes. When I picked you up you seemed very together, the way you always do. Then when we walked into this place I thought you would faint. Now you're lit up like Times Square. Don't get me wrong, I'm not complaining; but are you *okay*?"

"Maybe a little jet-lagged," Eileen answered. "Don't worry. I'll be fine at the meeting tomorrow."

"I know you will be. I know what a trooper you are. That's not the point. I'm your friend, remember?"

Eileen made a gesture of impatience. "Oh, please stop saying that."

"Have I been saying it a lot? Sorry." He stiffened. "I thought that was the way you wanted things."

"It is, but— oh, Alan, I'm sorry. I didn't mean to hurt your feelings. It's just that the word *friend* is a little tainted for me." She looked daggers at the back of the head of the blonde in the blue scarf. The stranger had said the scarf was for a friend— some friend. "You used the word *pals* before," Eileen continued. "I like that better than *friends*."

She took a sip and then a gulp from her glass. She listened to the rise and fall of conversation in the elegant room. A few tables away, a woman said, "Oh, bloody damn," in rounded British tones, and Eileen thought, I know just how she feels.

The stranger put his hands on the shoulders of the scarf-flaunting blonde. Eileen's shoulders stung sweetly with the memory of his fingers pressing into her flesh. She leaned across the table and lightly stroked back Alan's fair hair. Did the stranger see her? What did he feel? She repeated the gesture.

"Twigs in my hair?" Alan joked.

"I just wanted to mess it up a little. You always style

it so perfectly. I guess something in me rebels at so much order."

"That's the whole point, you see. Trying to disturb ladies like you." He peered at Eileen. He shook his head. "You're a very confusing human being, you know. I hope—"

Eileen leaned forward intimately. Did the stranger see? "You hope what?" she intoned breathily.

"I hope you're not toying with me, baby, that's all. Planning on giving me a dose of my own medicine and then thumbing your nose at me."

The stranger suddenly leaned back and laughed his merry laugh, as though his companion had just uttered the wittiest words ever spoken. For a moment Eileen could not speak. Then Alan's message penetrated her brain. She felt her cheeks burst into color to rival the flame of her dress.

"Alan—" she began. The words would not come. She gave her head a little shake, as though to jar the words loose. The pungent smell of French cigarette tobacco came drifting her way and abruptly she asked, "Do you have a cigarette?"

"Martinis? Cigarettes? Are you really Eileen Connor? I quit smoking five years ago, baby. Lost a big match at my club because my wind let me down, and that was the end of the romance between Alan Scott and Pall Malls. But I'll get you a pack if you like—even though I disapprove." He signaled for the waiter.

"No, never mind. Thank you. Just a momentary madness. Everything is momentary madness tonight. Alan, I'm sorry, I'm just not myself. I didn't sleep well last night, and—I'm sorry." She drained her martini glass. "Would you mind awfully if we skipped dinner? I honestly don't think I can eat. We could go to the Chat d'Or another night."

His face crumpled. He looked like a small boy who'd just been informed that some promised treat was being withdrawn. "Is there something you'd rather eat than fondue? You've got to have something. You look like you're going to melt away. Thin may be beautiful, but there are limits."

"I don't want to hurt you," Eileen said, honestly. "And I'm kind of flaky tonight. I might, you know, give you the wrong idea."

"I can take care of myself. I may not be a man of steel, but I'm not made of rose petals, either. Just as long as I know you're not deliberately trying to knock the wind out of my sails. Malice aforethought, as the legal boys put it, is my undoing." He gave Eileen a wry grin. "I once had a wife who specialized in that. It's been my Achilles' heel ever since."

"I didn't know you'd ever been married."

"It's not general knowledge around the Marsden Agency. It was way back in the Dark Ages—college. You've got a divorce behind you, too, don't you?"

"Last year. And I know just what you mean. I think I can take almost anything from men—except the sort of pain my ex-husband specialized in handing out."

"And what was that?" Alan asked gently.

Eileen glanced covertly at the stranger and his blonde companion. "He was unfaithful," she said, her voice growing small and quiet.

Alan signaled for the waiter. "What kind of host am I, letting you sit there with an empty glass? What do you say to another round? Maybe it'll spark your appetite."

"Or knock me out flat! Okay, what's to lose?"

Alan ordered. Then he said to Eileen, "Who could be unfaithful to you?"

"Oh, Alan," Eileen retorted boldly, "don't hand me that line. Everyone knows what a womanizer you are." For a moment she was afraid she'd gone too far, but he merely laughed. Nicely.

"Proud of the title, ma'am," he said. "I happen to be a man who genuinely likes women—lots of women. But playing the field when you're unattached is a very different thing from being unfaithful."

"What do you mean?" Eileen asked.

"I mean I never try to fool anybody. The women I go out with know just what I am—and they can take it or leave it. If I ever really fall in love again, that'll be a different matter. I was faithful to my wife, even when the marriage was sliding downhill as fast as an avalanche. I could be faithful again. Hell, I'd probably want to be faithful if I cared that much for someone."

The waiter brought fresh drinks. Eileen sipped the sweet-tart coldness of her martini and nodded her approval. "The women you go out with," she asked, "do they go out with other men, too? Don't you ever get jealous?"

"Sometimes I wish I did," the blond account executive admitted a little sadly. "But I'm just not that emotionally involved. To tell you the absolute truth, sometimes when I'm in bed with a woman, I wish I were home reading a good book."

Eileen felt her famous flush rising. "Oh, Alan!" Then she laughed. "Well, I can recommend lots of good books any time you want to change your way of living."

"I'd take your recommendation any day," Alan said. "You're a wise little thing, I suspect. I'm really enjoying talking with you, baby. I mean, *pal*."

The stranger's blond companion stood up. The stranger stood out of politeness, then sat down. Eileen didn't need to read the script to deduce that the blonde was heading for the ladies' room. The table where Eileen and Alan were sitting was in her path, and as the other woman came closer, Eileen thought the pretty, ivory face looked familiar. Yes, she was certain of it now. But where could she have seen her?

"You look," Alan commented, "as though you've seen a ghost. Trying to place that long blond drink of water? Palm Beach, 1959, maybe?"

Eileen was totally startled. "Alan!"

"I'm not the blockhead I sometimes appear to be," he said. His voice was in no way reproachful. It's been pretty obvious for about the last half-hour that I had at best fifty percent of your attention. Which isn't a complaint. Fifty percent of Eileen Connor is more interesting than a hundred percent of most of the women I know. But now that it's out in the open, who is she?"

Eileen shook her head. "I honestly don't remember. But you didn't mean it, did you, about her being a drink of water? She's very pretty."

"If you like that very heavily made-up model-type beauty."

"Which I guess is exactly what most men do like," Eileen stated. She aimed for ironic laughter but didn't get there.

"Hey." Alan put his hand over hers. "You're too beautiful and too terrific to be jealous. Look, she has a kind of slick attractiveness, but I think most men prefer your vivacious kind of looks. With that new haircut and your new wardrobe, you can probably have— Hey, what is it? What's wrong?"

The blonde was sitting down with the stranger again. With a sinking heart Eileen suddenly realized where she'd seen the blonde before.

She was a stewardess. Of all the professions on earth, she was in the one that reverberated most darkly in Eileen's heart. Eileen took another look. She was positive now. The woman had been a member of Vee Lenke's crew. That's where Eileen had seen her before—on her Swissair flight to Geneva.

Like her ex-husband, Keith, the stranger clearly preferred the company of an air hostess to that of Eileen.

Eileen was totally drained. She had no more interest in trying to make the stranger jealous. She had no more interest in making conversation with Alan. She felt as though her body had been pummeled. Her mouth tasted dry and too sweet, as if she were coming down with the flu.

She gathered herself together long enough to make a little speech to Alan. "We've got a big day tomorrow. I really want to be in shape. I've just got to go upstairs and crawl into bed. If I get hungry I'll order something from room service. I won't be any fun for you if we go out to dinner. And, quite honestly, I don't think I'll be able to enjoy myself." She put her hand on his sleeve and jiggled his cufflink. She looked up at his boyish blue eyes. "I really do like you, and I'm glad we're working together, and I'm sorry to be such a pill. I'm not proud of myself tonight, believe me."

She rose, planted a kiss on the top of his head before he had a chance to stand up, and whisked herself out through the revolving door.

chapter 7

DEAR TALL STRANGER,

You will never see this letter, but I have to write it anyway. Maybe if I put all my thoughts about you in one place I can somehow get free of them. I think I have to get free of them in order to be able to live my life as something other than a half-crazed creature.

But do I really want to be free of you?

I know now what novels mean when they talk about a heroine being "awakened." It's as though I was half asleep all my life and you woke me up. I don't want to go back to sleep. But what's the point in being awake if you're not there?

I thought I loved my husband. I thought I hated him. But the feelings I have toward you are so strong that I realize what I felt for him was neither love nor hate.

He was the rehearsal. You are the play. The play's the thing, isn't that what Shakespeare said?

Sorry if I'm rambling a bit. I had tee martoonies, as they say on the Avenue of President Madison. And it's late, and I'm still jet-lagged, and I haven't eaten, and I was supposed to sleep only there wasn't any peace in it, and now I'm sitting at my desk looking out at the Lake, and there's a toenail sliver of moon, and the Old Town looks like a Christmas tree in the darkness, and I miss my parents in a way and would like to call them only it would scare them half to death, and I was unfair to a decent man tonight (Alan Scott) because of you, EVERYTHING BECAUSE OF YOU.

You see, what you did was in a way much worse than what my husband did, because he only saw me asleep but you saw me AWAKE. You saw the real Eileen, the best Eileen there can be, and you didn't want her.

WHY?

Why did you come into my life and scoop me up and yell at me and tease me and kiss me kiss me kiss me and make me laugh and feel so wonderful so full and awake AND THEN NEVER COME BACK?

Until I saw you tonight in the Richemond Bar I had a tiny pocket of hope. I thought, maybe you got delayed somehow last night and got to the Chandelier later than I did, I mean maybe your taxi had a flat tire or something like that. Or maybe you got there early and when I was a few minutes late it seemed like a lot of minutes late, and so you left before I showed up. But then I saw you with that blonde, and the scarf from you around her neck, and I knew. She's the one you really care for. I was a joke.

You shouldn't have done it. I was getting to feel pretty good about life again before I met you. I might have met another man and been pretty happy with him. Maybe I could have liked Alan in a different way (though probably not). Or maybe my friend Vee's brother would have turned out to be someone interesting (though her descriptions of him make me nervous somehow). But I met you instead and who will match up to you?

No one will be as wonderful. No one will be as terrible.

Okay, I will never again think a second-rate man is really a first-rate man, so maybe you did a good thing for me. But do I really believe that?

I think my life is going to be very lonely.

I truly hate you.

I don't understand you.

Why did you seem so taken with me?

Why do I still think you're wonderful?

Why do I still want you?

I feel calmer for writing this letter. I also feel silly. I'm a grown-up woman. A divorcee. And I know I'm acting seventeen.

I guess because when I was seventeen I first dreamed about finding a man like you. The dream in the cave—I think I always saw your face in that dream. You were always the one who knew the things I needed to know, the secret of life. And then when I was eighteen I met Keith. I forgot about you. I made myself forget about you. I made myself think that Keith was really It, that I was really lucky to have found him. And he took me to New York, and I had much too much on my mind to give you a thought.

Except that now and then I dreamed about the cave.

My mother says I analyze too much, and maybe she's right. Only sometimes analysis helps, even when it hurts.

I guess that's all I have to say. In a way, even though you and your "friend" are probably laughing at me, I almost hope you know how deeply you got to me. At least I've *felt* love now, the real thing, and real hate too, for whatever that's worth.

I might never have felt those things. That would have been worse than what I'm feeling now.

Pretty philosophical, aren't I? I wonder if it will last.

DAMN YOU.

DAMN YOU GARY COOPER.

Love and hate,
Little One

chapter 8

"ALAN," EILEEN BEGAN, "about last night—"

They were sitting at the desk in her hotel room. The Mont Blanc presentation was spread out in front of them. The ruins of a delicious room service breakfast languished on a table to one side. In the far distance, the Lake manifested its grand blue mass. For the past hour Eileen and Alan had discussed work, food, and view—without a mention of the previous evening. Now the subject was up for grabs. Eileen looked anxiously at her colleague.

"Never mind," he said gently. "Please don't think you owe me any explanations. To tell you the truth, I ended up grabbing a sandwich at a little café down the street, and then I tumbled into bed. Quite alone. So here we both are, bright-eyed and bushy-tailed, ready to do our best by old man Marsden."

Eileen almost sighed with relief. Alan was a sweetheart to let her off the hook so easily. "I do hope we land that account," she said, ever so happy to conspire to discuss something neutral and safe. "When I think of what our hotel bills will cost Mr. Marsden—"

"Tax deductible," Alan assured her. "Not to worry. Shall I phone room service and have them send up some more melon? Another round of *croissants*?"

"Oh, I couldn't. I'm stuffed. Anyway, we ought to get going in a minute. I don't want to keep *Monsieur* Longemalle waiting."

"I don't believe it. Did I really hear those words from the late Ms. Eileen Connor?"

"Well, you have to be on time in Switzerland, don't you?" For a dark moment, Eileen remembered the night when she hadn't been on time—and when the tall stranger hadn't shown up at all. Then she reaffirmed the mental resolve she'd arrived at after finishing her letter to him the night before. She wasn't going to think about him. She wasn't going to remember the sweet moments; she wasn't going to relive the agonizing moments. He was no longer welcome in her thoughts, period and end of sentence.

Half an hour later, precisely at ten o'clock, they were exchanging greetings with Jean-Claude Longemalle and his two most important underlings at the Mont Blanc watch company: advertising director Roger St. Denis and the vice-president in charge of the new American sales program, Ernst Vogt. Longemalle, Eileen noted, had the burnished air of a European elder statesman, from his full head of silvery hair to the glinting gold housing on his vest-pocket watch. St. Denis and Vogt were in their thirties—contemporaries of Alan Scott's—and virtually indistinguishable in dress and bearing from their American counterparts whom Eileen had met.

Eileen wasn't at all surprised that *Monsieur* Longemalle kissed the hand she offered him, and that the other two men firmly shook her hand. There was a clear generation gap here. She thanked Longemalle for the flowers he'd sent her. He beamed and then asked, eyes twinkling: "It's still all right to send flowers to an American woman? I haven't insulted your politics? My two colleagues here," gesturing at St. Denis and Vogt, "think I'm terribly out of step."

"If my independence can be compromised by a few flowers," she shot back, "it must be a pretty feeble specimen."

The three Swiss laughed. Alan, who spoke no French at all, said to her, "Now I know what it would be like to watch a great French comedy film and have the subtitles suddenly stop. Translate, please?"

Shortly the group moved on to a conference room. Like everything else Eileen had seen since she entered the company's headquarters, the room was very traditional, very

European, very elegant. As she looked at the large oak conference table and the heavy leather chairs, she thought, this room is dressed like *Monsieur* Longemalle. Or perhaps he's dressed like it?

Eileen and Alan set up their presentation. Eileen's work quickly grew intense. The two younger men from the Mont Blanc firm spoke quite good English—though even Vogt, who'd spent a year at an American prep school, missed some of the slang and wordplay so important in ads; and *Monsieur* Longemalle, fluent in German, Italian, the Romansh dialect of Switzerland, and of course French, spoke virtually no English.

"When you reach the peak, you're ready for a Mont Blanc." Ernst Vogt, looking rather like an overgrown Swiss schoolboy trying to memorize a lesson, kept repeating the words. Finally his tanned face creased with pleasure, and he emphatically nodded his approval. "It works," he said. "I like it. I congratulate you, *Monsieur* Scott. And you, *Mademoiselle* Connor."

Roger St. Denis chewed on the words a little longer. "*Quand vous arrivez en haut*," he translated aloud. "Is that a fair rendition, *Mademoiselle* Connor?"

"'When you arrive at the top,'" she said for Alan's benefit. "A bit of the nuance is lost, perhaps, but yes, *monsieur*, that's the essence of the message."

"And you think that will appeal to—shall I be frank?— the snob instinct in the American buyer?"

"Not just that," Alan interjected. "The Mont Blanc watch should be associated with genuine achievement, not with mere status. We think that catch phrase will appeal to those who had to work their way up in the world, not just those born at the top."

"I like it," Ernst Vogt stressed again.

"And I think it sounds a bit—sweaty," St. Denis said. "Don't you think you are perhaps biased in its favor because you are a mountain climber?" He turned to his American guests and explained, "Ernst Vogt holds the record, among other things, for climbing Mont Salève."

Unthinkingly Alan said, "I thought that Le Salève was a hill that tourists could walk up in a couple of hours."

"There is a path, yes," Eileen said hastily, "but there's also a very difficult rocky face that's not at all for tourists. In fact—correct me if I'm wrong, *Monsieur* Vogt—I believe the art of *varappe*, of rock climbing with ropes, got its name from the practice grounds of Le Salève where climbing as a sport originated."

For the first time in many minutes, company president Jean-Claude Longemalle entered into the conversation. Up until now, he had appeared—in Eileen's view—to be interested in watching his two subordinates engage in a power play. Now he made it clear that all real power resided in him—all real power and all real charm.

He made a little bow in Eileen's direction and said, "You seem to have gone to some trouble, *mademoiselle*, to learn about Geneva. That's very flattering to those of us who love this city. Too many Americans seem to think it's merely a stopping point between Paris and Rome, a shopping center for cheese and chocolate. Tell me, *mademoiselle*, are you the one who dreamed up this slogan with which to sell Mont Blanc watches?"

Eileen flushed. She knew perfectly well that Longemalle was aware she was a secretary, not a copy writer. She wondered what he was getting at. "I wish I were capable of putting words together that way," she said, with all the lightness she could conjure.

Longemalle bowed again. "You are being diplomatic. You do not wish to be disloyal to your company. Very commendable. I wish all my employees were committed to me and my company in that way. But here is my point." He looked at each face in the room. "She could not have come up with that slogan because she knows too much about Geneva." Alan shifted uncomfortably in his big leather chair. Longemalle directed Eileen, "Explain to your colleague."

Eileen's mouth was dry. The relaxed meeting of Americans and Swiss had suddenly turned very tense. She said to Alan, "I think what *Monsieur* Longemalle means is that since Mont Blanc is actually in France, not in Switzerland, it might be better not to stress the mountain in the advertising material. It somehow takes away from the Swiss-ness of the watches."

Ernst Vogt translated for Longemalle as Eileen spoke to Alan, and Longemalle punctuated her explanation with nods of agreement.

"But the fact remains," Alan insisted, "that the name of the watches is Mont Blanc—not Le Salève or anything else. And Mont Blanc is a name that connotes rare achievement."

Eileen half-expected Longemalle to react with irritation to Alan's statement, but instead the silver-haired company president nodded yet more vigorously. His rich mane of hair flopped half a beat out of step, like a neophyte drummer trying to keep up with the band. "The truth of the matter is," he said, "that Mont Blanc remains the name of the company only because of complex financial and legal arrangements. The company might more appropriately be called Longemalle Watches. Though," shrugging his distaste, "we might then run the risk of being confused—in untutored minds—with another manufacturer of watches with a similiar name."

What an ego! Eileen thought, and prayed that the thought didn't show. She looked at Alan Scott. The ball was clearly in his court.

"Well, clearly, *monsieur*, we have to scrap this theme and come up with another. I have every hope that we'll find a slogan more to your liking." Alan rummaged around in his mind and said, "Here's one just off the top of my head. 'Mont Blanc watches. For the time of your life.'"

Longemalle wrinkled his patrician nose. "It makes me think of a whiskey commercial."

"Or beer," chimed in Roger St. Denis. Eileen began to get the feeling that St. Denis would say nearly anything to curry favor with his employer, no matter at whose expense.

"These are serious times we live in," Longemalle said. "Money is tight—even at the top. Even," he added, as if trying to soften the mood, "at the top of Mont Blanc. We will not sell watches in America by playing the snob or being cutesy." He looked at Eileen in a way that made her both glad and sorry that she had worn her revealing new cerise-trimmed white silk shirt to pep up her maroon wool suit. "Perhaps you would do well, *Monsieur* Scott, to let *Mademoiselle* Connor turn her hand to this project instead of sending it back to your 'creative geniuses.' I hope I do not offend you?"

"No one can offend me by admiring *Mademoiselle* Connor," Alan said, and a blushing Eileen was glad that Ernst Vogt and not she had the responsibility of translating the sentence for *Monsieur* Longemalle.

After a few amenities, Jean-Claude Longemalle stood up. The meeting was over. No further mention was made of a tour of the watch factory. No one asked Alan Scott if he planned to play much tennis in Geneva. The Swiss very evidently thought that Alan and Eileen should return to their bunker and produce, produce, produce.

Alan didn't say a word to Eileen as the elevator descended from the top of the Mont Blanc building. Not until they were safely out on the street, in neutral territory, did he let loose. Then he *really* let loose. "That two-bit tyrant," he fumed, he shouted. He rolled up the Mont Blanc presentation and jammed it into a public waste bin. "That dyed-haired egomaniac! I know his type. Oh, do I know them. Whatever you bring them the first time around has to be scrapped because they can't stand the thought that anyone has ideas but themselves. Ten meetings and a barrel of sweat later, you bring them virtually the same thing and they love it because they think they've had a hand in creating it."

"Take it easy, Alan." Eileen put a cautionary hand on his arm as they hurried down the winter-bright streets of the city.

"Easy? I haven't started! Damn that smarmy, slimy, hand-kissing creep. As for those two undertakers he has working for him—"

"Ernst Vogt isn't so bad. I think he liked what we did."

"Sure he liked it. But did he defend it? The moment there was trouble, he shut up like a clam. Office politics—it's the pits! That's what we're caught in the middle of, you know. There's a faction that doesn't want to sell in America, and we're the jam in that uneasy sandwich. Speaking of which—let's go have lunch. A four-martini lunch." He stopped dead and looked around. "Where are we, anyway?"

"Near the Palace of Nations."

"Oh, great. Oh, terrific. Let's go have a nice long look at Mont Blanc. Blasted mountain— Let's go anywhere else. Is that an empty cab? Taxi! In you go, baby. Tell the driver where we want to go."

Eileen leaned forward. "The Old Town," she instructed the driver. "The Chandelier." Was she being foolish? she wondered a moment later. Was she risking an unpleasant encounter with a man she genuinely did not want to see? No, she decided, the Chandelier was probably the last restaurant in Geneva that the tall stranger would go to today. If by some chance she did see him, she wouldn't feel a thing—so she sternly programmed herself. The important thing was that the Chandelier was a charming restaurant with a well-stocked bar. And Alan Scott had very great need just now of such a place.

As she had hoped and expected, the beauty of the Old Town took Alan out of his foul mood. "It's like Chinatown in New York," he marveled. "The crooked little streets. You were right about my being a person who doesn't always look, but who could be immune to this place?"

As they sat down at the bar inside the Chandelier, Alan gave Eileen a grateful smile. "Thanks for letting me blow off steam that way. And just for being here. You're a fantastic support. I don't know how much of a career you want in advertising, but I'm going to put every possible good word in for you with old man Marsden. What are you drinking? A martini?"

"Not at noon. It'd be all over for me. I'll have a glass of white wine. Have you tried the Swiss white wine yet? It's so clear and crisp—very refreshing."

"Maybe tonight at dinner. We are dining together, aren't we, pal? Meanwhile I need all the alcohol I can get into my veins." He ordered wine for Eileen and a martini for himself.

After the drinks came Eileen asked, "What do we do now? Can we pull this deal off?"

"Sure, baby, a snap," Alan said automatically. Then he grinned ruefully and said, "I don't know."

"Are you going to call Mr. Marsden? Does this go back to a copy writer and art director now?"

"That's the trouble," Alan said. "That's the way things are usually done—but there isn't time. I just have a feeling, Eileen, that if we don't come up with a new approach in the next couple of days, we're going to lose the momentum—and the account. Frankly, I'm counting on you."

"What do you mean?"

"Longemalle is very taken with you, I think. He trusts you, somehow. I think he'd look twice as favorably at something coming from you as at something coming from the bright boys—or from me."

Eileen quaffed wine. Her mouth instantly felt invigorated. "But I don't know how to put together a presentation."

"Oh, you don't have to do a whole presentation. If you could just come up with an approach, a catch phrase, a theme— Then, if Longemalle goes for it, we can probably send for a creative group to dummy up some new ads. You have an advantage over anyone back in New York, you see. You've met Longemalle. You've seen his office. You seem to have a grasp of this city and this country. Did you go to school here or something?"

"I was never in Switzerland before at all," Eileen laughed. "But I did travel a lot when I was a kid—mostly in France and Germany and Italy and the Middle East a little—and my parents always made us read guidebooks before we started out and maybe some novels set in the places we were going to. Some Air Force people just stuck to the base, but my mother would always take me to visit the museums and churches and markets and streets wherever we traveled, and she thought I'd enjoy it more if I read up ahead of time. So, to finish up this rather windy answer to your question, I read up on Geneva before we came over. That's all. And did a little exploring the day before you got here."

Alan drained his glass. "I'm ready for another. How about you?"

"No, I'm fine, thanks. I guess I have to do some hard thinking this afternoon, so I'd better be in shape." She grinned. "Ironic, isn't it? The late Eileen Connor has to come up with the ultimate phrase about watches. Would anyone back at the office believe it?"

"How about 'Better late then never,'" Alan teased. "Do you think Monsieur Longemalle would go for that?"

Eileen flashed back to the night—so recently, so long ago—when she'd waited in vain for the tall stranger to appear at this bar. For a moment her studied indifference evaporated and she dwelled in a state of pure pain. "'Better never than late,'" she muttered.

Oh, why had she chosen the Chandelier as the place to have lunch? Too late, she realized that she'd chosen it precisely so she could feel the pain she was feeling. The trouble was, the pain really hurt. "I think I will have more wine," she said.

chapter 9

"TIME," EILEEN EXCLAIMED, pacing the floor of her elegant, pale hotel room. "Time, where is thy sting?" She looked at her worn old leather-encased traveling alarm clock. "Talk to me," she begged it. "Yield your secrets." She walked over to the flower arrangement that Monsieur Longemalle had sent her the day of her arrival. The freesia were withering; their perfume was no longer intense. "Time kills all things," Eileen declared, rearranging a tulip and a daisy, "and it's going to kill me."

The notepad on her desk was covered with doodles and crossed-out words. She had not come up with a single phrase she considered useful. She sat down at her desk again, but she knew she was finished for the moment. Her mind would produce nothing except horrible puns. *You have to hand it to your Mont Blanc watch, it's always on time. Our watch has your number. Face it, you need a Mont Blanc watch. If you want to wind up your affairs, get a Mont Blanc watch.*

The telephone rang. Alan, she supposed, wanting to check on her progress.

Instead she heard the warm, eager tones of Vee Lenke's voice. "Eileen? Hi. I wondered if we could rearrange our plans. I've got to exchange trips with a member of my crew who needs to have the weekend free to handle some kind of family crisis. So I'm here today and tomorrow. Do you suppose—I know this is terribly last minute—but do you suppose you could come up to Vevey this evening? If you caught the six o'clock train, you'd be in good time for

65

dinner, and Matt could drive you back later on. Do say yes.
I'm so eager to have you meet everyone and see this place."

"Vee, I'd love to," Eileen answered. "We've had a work
snag, and I've been doing some thinking—and, well, I have
to get away from it for a couple of hours or I'm not going
to have the kind of breakthrough I have to have. But I told
Alan Scott—he's the account supervisor I'm working
with—that I'd have dinner with him."

"You can have dinner with him any night, can't you?"

"Yes—but he's pretty anxious about our work, and I
hate to desert him."

"Invite him to come along, then." Vee's voice had a
certain reluctance as she issued the invitation, and Eileen
realized with an inward sigh that Vee hadn't yet given up
her hopes of making a match between her brother and Eileen
and therefore didn't want Eileen to have an escort.

"Oh, it'll be too much trouble for you," Eileen said.
"What about tomorrow night?"

"Matt is having dinner with one of his clients. Didn't
you say you were working on a campaign for the Mont
Blanc watch company? Matt has just been commissioned
to design a vacation home for Jean-Claude Longemalle and
his new wife. Régine Longemalle is quite the social butterfly, don't you know, and she's summoned Matt for tomorrow night. I just hope," she added meaningfully, sounding more like a possessive wife or a worrying mother than
Eileen's idea of a sister, "that her husband will be home.
So do come tonight, with your Alan Scott. It's just another
cup of water in the soup."

"Monsieur Longemalle recently got married?" Eileen
was having trouble picturing the willful company president
as a bridegroom. It wasn't just that he was in his mid-
seventies, it was that he seemed too wrapped up in business
and self-obsessed to have pursued a woman to the altar.

"For the fifth time, my dear," Vee Lenke announced
gleefully. "He's a bit of a scandal, our silver-maned old
warhorse is. Come tonight and we'll fill you in on all the
local gossip. Who knows? Maybe you'll pick up some in-

sight that will help you in dealing with him."

As usual, Eileen was reluctant to say no to her enthusiastic new friend. "All right," she decided. "I'm sure Alan
will be thrilled to take his mind off work. Unless you hear
back from me, we'll be on that six o'clock train. How do
we get to your house from the station?"

"It's a short but complicated walk. It'll take me less time
to meet you than to give you directions. Anyway, it's our
housekeeper's day off, and I'm the sort of cook who always
needs to make a last-minute dash into the shops."

"Can I bring you anything from the big city?"

"Just your sweet American self," the air hostess said.
"Oh, by the way, please wear jeans or some such. We're
super casual up here."

An hour later Alan was saying to Eileen, "This train
reminds me of the little engine that could."

They were chugging their way along a winding, hilly
route that afforded frequent flashes of the famous Lake.
The train was loaded to capacity and seemed to belly-ache
its way up the inclines.

"I guess this is the local equivalent of the five-forty-
seven to Scarsdale," Eileen commented. Men with brief-
cases on their laps and newspapers in front of their faces
filled most of the worn gray leather seats.

"Do you think you'd like that life?" Alan asked. "Being
a commuter? Or a commuter's wife? House, station wagon,
and two-point-four kids in Westchester County?"

"You make it sound so dreadful. Like part of some em-
barrassing statistic," Eileen protested. She shook her head.
"I don't know what I want anymore. Or maybe I do know
but I can't admit it to myself. How about you?"

Alan looked out the window for a moment. The train
sounded its mournful whistle. A conductor called out the
next station stop, "Nyon! Nyon!"

"I guess it's city life for me," he said finally. "This kind
of view is terrific to look at now and then, but I think I'd
get nervous living with a lot of trees around. And I can't
stand the idea of being someplace that closes up at eleven

o'clock at night. I want to know I can find a newspaper or a drink of coffee or company any hour of the day or night. Hey, baby, what's the matter? Did I say something wrong?"

"No, nothing," she said hastily. Despite all her determination to scalpel him out of her thoughts, the stranger still had root in her mind. She couldn't help thinking as Alan talked that the stranger and she would have exactly identical notions on how to live. She didn't know what his notions were. At the moment she didn't even know what her own notions were. Still she was sure that their notions were twinned.

"You look too pretty to frown," Alan told her, sweetly but inanely. "If a pal is permitted to say such things to a pal." She was wearing the crimson velvet jeans and the pink turtleneck sweater that the stranger had picked out.

"You look pretty pretty yourself," she returned, eying Alan's tattersall shirt, pale blue shetland sweater, khaki pants, and sneakers. "The all-American preppie."

Suddenly she couldn't bear their conversation. Alan Scott was a decent man, a good pal, an agreeable enough colleague; but she couldn't help seeing him as basically weak. That weakness grated on her. She didn't mind having to help him out with the Mont Blanc business—in fact, she rather welcomed the challenge; she didn't mind being his tour guide and entertainment director. Sometimes she just minded his aura.

She told him she had a slight headache and wanted to take a nap. He nodded sympathetically. She leaned back into the rhythm of the train. She shut her eyes. She started to dream of the cave. *No!* her mind protested. Dreaming of the cave meant dreaming of the stranger. And dreaming of the stranger meant disaster.

Her mood improved when the train arrived in Vevey and she saw Vee. Her stewardess friend was wearing paint-splotched Levis, a sweater that had to have been her husband's, and an enormous smile of welcome. Eileen noted with relief that Vee seemed to like Alan at once—not that

Eileen could imagine Vee disliking anyone but an ogre.

"Your hair!" Vee suddenly burbled to Eileen, as they walked past a bakery emitting the aroma of fresh crusty bread. "You cut it! Marvelous!" She linked arms with Eileen. "I think my adopted country agrees with you. Oh, do you mind if we just nip in to this market here? I need some endive. Matt announced tonight that a salad without endive wasn't worth having, and when Matt announces I move. Do you have a sister, Alan? Do you boss her mercilessly?"

"I have an older sister who still beats me up," Alan answered. "Maybe your brother and I could do a sister-swap sometime. I'd love to have someone to boss. I don't think I ever even had a puppy that obeyed me."

Vee bought endive, and some extra cream, and the trio started up a hill that led away from town. Eileen shivered. The air was chillier than in Geneva; there was a real winter bite.

"Is Marie still awake?" she asked Vee. "I'm dying to meet her."

"She's awake, all right. She's given up sleeping this week. I think she's cutting a two-year molar. I *hope* she is. If she's just simply given up sleeping, I'm going to kill myself." This startling pronouncement was delivered with such cheeriness that Eileen could only smile. Vee was quite a person, she decided. She hoped that when she was forty herself she would have Vee's figure and looks. She hoped that when she was a mother she would have Vee's good-humored competence and devotion.

Vee's house was a ramble of old stone, surrounded by terraced vineyards. As Vee pushed open the heavy, carved wooden door, little Marie came running out and leaped into her mother's arms. The red-haired sprite peered at Eileen and Alan. She squiggled around to put her cheek close to her mother's. "Hi or *bon soir*, mama?" she asked.

"These are 'hi' people, honey," she said.

"Hi hi hi people," Marie chirped.

"Is she really bilingual?" Alan asked.

"Oh, it's all mixed up," Vee announced. "In another year she'll either be able to go to work at the U.N. as an interpreter—or not speak anything at all."

"Down, mama," Marie ordered, and Vee obediently set her pajama-clad offspring on the floor.

"Go tell Papa and Uncle Matt that we're here," Vee told her. She took Eileen's and Alan's coats. "Come into the living room, you two. Let me get you something to drink. We've got everything from Southern Comfort to Polish buffalo grass vodka, so just name it."

"I'd like to try some of your wine," Eileen said, and Alan seconded the suggestion. As Vee busied herself at a very serious-looking bar, Eileen took in the room. There was a feeling of massiveness and density about it—low ceilings, a huge fireplace with a crackling blaze, shuttered windows—outrageously, and beautifully, offset by streamlined modern furniture and huge, brilliant abstract paintings that were the very embodiment of intelligent energy.

"What a room!" she gasped. She turned to Alan, who was following her darting gaze. "You wanted to know how I'd like to live? This is how I'd like to live. With all these contrasts—the dark and the bright, the ancient and the futuristic. This room is all and everything. Vee, who did these paintings? Who put this room together?"

"I did," answered a man's voice that sent shivers down Eileen's back.

She turned toward the source of the sound.

"My brother, Matt Edwards," Vee was saying.

Eileen knew him by another name.

The tall stranger.

chapter 10

"How do you do?" Eileen heard herself manage to say. She did not offer her hand, though ordinarily she liked shaking hands when she was introduced to someone. Speaking to him was one thing; touching him was quite another. She would have died, she was sure of it. She would simply have crumpled up on the bright Scandinavian rug.

"How do you do?" he echoed with perfect politeness, then turned to Alan.

Eileen was elated. She was shattered. She wanted to sing. She wanted to scream. Her heart embodied as many contrasting emotions and ideas as the room they were standing in embodied.

She loved him. She hated him. She wanted to forgive him. She wanted to punish him. Oh, glorious, unbearable stew of emotions.

At least I'm alive, she thought. No matter how miserable I am when he's near me, I'm alive.

"So you like this room, do you?" Matt coolly asked Eileen. "You like my paintings? My sister thinks they're awful, meaningless scrawls. She only keeps them up to humor me."

"Oh, Matt," Vee protested. "It's not that I don't admire your paintings. But they're so full of anger."

"Every time a woman disappoints me, I take to my easel," Matt said. "I have enough paintings to fill a gallery."

"And what about the women you disappoint?" Eileen

asked, striving to match his offhand tone. "How do they usually express their anger? By driving in demolition derbies?"

Her timing was perfect. Vee chortled. "Oh, Eileen, that was delicious," she cried. "I've waited thirty years for someone to put Matt down that way." She stood up, walked over to her brother, and ruffled his dark hair. "And if you do it again, you won't get any dinner!" she declared mock-threateningly to Eileen. "Well, hello! Here is the famous husband."

Eileen stood up to greet her host. She realized at once why Vee Lenke appeared to be such a happy woman. Tall, broad-shouldered, balding Pierre Lenke radiated warmth and attentiveness. It didn't hurt his image any, of course, that his adorable daughter was sitting on his shoulders, tugging at what hair he had, and saying, "*Papa mon cheval. Papa mon cheval.*"

"I know," Alan interrupted, as Eileen started to translate. "I have a two-year old nephew. Some things are universal. She's saying 'Daddy is my horsie,' right?"

"Right."

Pierre gently set his daughter down and poured himself a glass of wine. "Welcome," he said, with only a trace of an accent. "Cheers."

"This is the most delicious wine I've ever drunk," Eileen declared honestly.

"Complex without being difficult. Subtly fruity with just a hint of astringency. Young but not juvenile," Alan incanted in perfect parody of the pretentious wine buff. Eileen noticed that Pierre and Vee seemed genuinely amused—and that Matt did not. Was it possible, she wondered, suddenly buoyant with hope, that he was jealous of Alan? Was it really, truly possible that he cared enough about her to be jealous?

Then a dark memory came swirling to the forefront of her mind. Waiting at the Chandelier. Waiting and waiting and waiting and waiting. Going home alone, crushed with disappointment. She must not be ruled by hope again. This man was poison.

She forced herself back into the concrete present, to the conversation at hand. "Do you make your living as a painter?" Alan was asking Matt. "I have some good connections with New York galleries," he added, with typical Madison Avenue brashness.

"That would be marvelous, wouldn't it?" Matt laughed. "Then all my follies with the female sex would be tax deductible, right?, since they're my inspiration. No, my painting is strictly an indulgence. A private madness. I make my living as an architect."

"Still," Alan persisted, "these canvases look like the sort of thing that are fetching big prices these days in New York."

Matt stood up. To Eileen's eyes, he didn't merely rise, he unfolded his great lean length and towered over the gathered company. He jammed his hands into the pockets of his heavy tan corduroy pants. His shoulders worked angrily under his charcoal-brown turtleneck sweater. "Not to be rude, Mr. Scott—"

"Alan," the account executive insisted genially.

"Not to be rude," Matt continued, "but I like to think that my canvases would be spurned by the New York galleries. The New York art scene these days is a cesspool. Corrupt, clannish, and just plain blind—that's what I think of most of the dealers on Madison Avenue and in Soho. Oh, here and there you see painters with integrity, with genius. I bought a Leland Bell self-portrait last week; you should see the glorious rage in it. No, I'm happier hanging on Vee's walls, tormenting her. Anyway, Mr. Scott, I don't live in New York and I don't share the current opinion that New York is the epicenter of the world, so why would your connections interest me?"

"Matt!" His adoring sister managed to muster a murmur of disapproval at the brusqueness of his little speech.

But Alan either didn't know or didn't care that he'd just

been royally snubbed. He merely shrugged and said, "That's what makes a horse race. One of our art directors had a show on Madison Avenue last year, and I happened to think it was terrific."

"Art director," Matt said, not bothering to hide the sneer in his voice. "I'd forgotten that in New York you can make a living that way."

For all her own dissatisfaction with New York, Eileen had a sudden urge to defend the city. The tall stranger—Matt, as she had to think of him now—was being unbearable. The intensity of his feelings was a wondrous thing to witness, but why shoot all that venom into poor, nice Alan? "How can an architect dismiss New York?" she shot back. "Is there a more stunning manmade creation on earth? Haven't you ever sailed into New York harbor at sunset, or flown over Manhattan? Seen those pure straight lines, all that beautifully arrogant upthrust, men and women reaching for the impossible? Your paintings have the same kind of energy I sometimes feel rising up out of the streets of Manhattan."

"Your enthusiasms are impressive," Matt Edwards said. "And I admire your eye. It would be a pleasure to look at some of my favorite structures with you—the Old Town of Geneva for instance."

Eileen felt as though she'd had a glass of ice water flung in her face. It was all she could do to keep from gasping.

"Eileen's already gone to the Old Town," Vee piped up, clearly proud of her friend's enterprising nature. "She told me."

"Did she?" Matt thundered. He took a sip—no, a swallow—from his wine glass. He focused his dark eyes on Eileen's flushed face and said, "I'm glad your visit there was so memorable that you saw fit to report it."

Vee and Pierre exchanged questioning glances. Alan shifted uncomfortably in his chair. Even Marie seemed to notice that something was askew in the room and she looked up from the game she was playing—trying to tie her father's shoelaces together.

"So," Matt observed to Eileen, abruptly as calm as he'd been roused, "you're one of those people who are addicted to New York."

"I said I thought it was beautiful," Eileen returned. "I didn't say I liked living there."

"Didn't you? It seems like the right place for you. And of course if you have ambitions in the advertising business," he said, sneering, "that's where the action is."

"And what part of the world do you grace with your presence?" Eileen asked as coolly as she knew how, determined not to let him know that his words stung like whips against her skin.

"No fixed abode," Matt answered. "I maintain an office in Boston, so my mail has someplace to go and my sister can always leave me a message, but basically I'm a vagabond. Known to hoteliers all over the world."

Eileen nodded. She felt miserable now. Her worst fears about the stranger were all coming true, one by one. Like her ex-husband, he had a taste for flashy blond air hostesses. Like her ex-husband, he was a wanderer.

She fixed her gaze on Alan. Why couldn't she, just once, fall for someone less toxic to her system? Alan had his flaws, but underneath the Madison Avenue patter there was a core of goodness.

Or was there? Wouldn't life with him grate against her nature even if it didn't threaten her serenity? She looked around the room, drinking in the thick walls, the spare furniture, the huge, brilliant, dynamic canvases. Alan would want to live in some conventional white-walled apartments with a few discreet, popular prints hanging at regular intervals, and a few discreet, popular friends positioned here and there on the sofas from Bloomingdale's.

Alan would never break her heart, but he would never awaken her heart.

With that amazing sense of timing children sometimes exhibit, Marie came toddling over to Eileen. 'Hi," she said, standing there, hands behind her back.

"Hi," Eileen said. She longed to swing the child up onto

her lap and hold her close, but she didn't want to frighten the red-headed pajama'd pixie. "Do you like stories?" she asked.

"Like stories!" Marie answered with clearly unfeigned enthusiasm.

"Do you like stories about kangaroos?"

"Kangaroos!" Marie echoed happily. Then she held up her arms for a hoist, and said, "Lap."

Eileen cuddled Marie and started to tell her the tale of Blippy, a kangaroo who belonged to a girl named Pamela. Pamela didn't like to carry things, and so she used Blippy's pouch as a pencil box, and a purse, and a shopping cart, and a suitcase—and finally she wanted to use Blippy to move a couch, only Blippy refused. The story had a refrain, and after a few rounds Eileen and Marie were saying more or less in unison:

"Ouch! My pouch! Not a couch!"

At the end of the story Marie clapped her hands and cried, "More! More pouch!"

"Ouch!" Eileen protested. "Not more couch!"

"What a marvelous story," Vee declared. "What's it called? Maybe I can find a copy for Marie."

"Oh, it's just something I made up," Eileen demurred.

"Hey, baby, I knew you were creative," Alan called out, "but I didn't know you were *that* creative. You ought to write it down, you know."

"I suppose you have connections in the publishing business," Matt Edwards observed acidly in Alan's direction.

"As it happens, I do. With the right illustrator, she could probably make a mint."

"Matt, show them the drawings you've done for Marie," Vee urged. "You wouldn't believe," she added to the room at large, "that they were done by the same soul responsible for these canvases."

But Matt wasn't moving. He was staring at Eileen. He was staring in particular at Eileen's cropped head.

"Your hair," he mouthed, so only Eileen could see. "You cut your hair."

She gave a little shrug. She wanted to take pleasure in the look of happy surprise on his face, but she couldn't. Apparently he'd been so jolted to see her in the Richemond Bar the previous evening and in his sister's living room tonight that he'd seen only the whole, not the parts. She'd had that experience herself, in reverse. At the Richemond she'd been so unpleasantly dazzled by the sight of a certain blue chiffon scarf that she hadn't immediately recognized the woman wearing it, hadn't even realized she knew her.

Right now she wished only that she hadn't had her hair cut. She loved the way it looked, and the ease of caring for it—just washing it and tossing it with her fingers; but she could not bear being the source of the satisfied look on Matt's lean face. Smug wretch, she thought. It must make the joke all the better for him that she had her hair cut to please him, and he never showed up to see it.

"Matt?" his sister was repeating. "Your drawings?"

"Drawings!" Marie echoed happily. "Drawings, please!"

His sister's urging was resistible; his niece's evidently was not. Matt traversed the room and started up a staircase.

As soon as he had disappeared, Vee said, "I love my brother too much to apologize for him, but I think I can properly explain him. He's had a rough time lately." She placed her hand over her heart.

"He's ill?" Alan asked solicitously. "But he looks like a mountain climber."

"No, no," Pierre laughed, "not that sort of trouble with the heart. The other kind—that does not kill you but only makes you wish you could die." He sighed dramatically, and everyone laughed.

Eileen said nothing. She just clutched little Marie closer. The child was such a lovely weight on her lap. And so warm. So very warm. So very, very warm...

... alarmingly warm!

"Uh oh," Eileen said to Vee. "I think we've got a damp baby here."

"Oh no, has she leaked all over you?" Vee exclaimed. She rushed over and took the baby into her arms. "I'll say

she has. Pierre, *chéri*, would you change the little darling
while I take Eileen upstairs and see if I can't find her another
pair of jeans? She's tinier than I am, but I'm sure I have
something that will fit her. Oh, Eileen, I'm sorry, your
beautiful velvet pants. Alan, sorry to desert you like this,
but there's the wine, just help yourself, and we'll be right
back."

Moments later the efficient Vee had installed Eileen in
the master bedroom with a damp towel for sponging herself
off and a pile of old jeans to choose from. Then she'd made
urgent gestures with her nose, declared that the bread she
was baking was burning up, and rushed out of the room.

Eileen took off her velvet jeans and laid them over a
chair to dry. She sponged the place on her thigh where the
baby had wet her. Dear Vee, she thought affectionately.
Such a good caretaker. She stood there in her sweater and
panties looking around at the room. The big old brass bed,
the antique wall sconces, the pale yellow and white striped
wallpaper, and a large oil portrait of Marie in her christening
dress all reflected the happy harmony she'd felt emanating
from Pierre and Marie.

She moved closer to the painting of the baby, looking
for a signature. Was it possible that this traditional, almost
sentimental, portrait had been painted by the creator of the
angry scrawls hanging below in the living room? Unlikely,
but something told her Matt had put his vibrant brush to
this canvas, too.

Suddenly a door was flung open behind her, and an
irritated male voice was saying, "Vee, I can't—"

She turned around. As she met Matt's stare, she realized
how little she was wearing. She felt her face color, but she
steeled herself against making the traditional gestures of
modesty, of outraged innocence. Dignity would make a
better fig leaf. She stood her ground. She said simply, "Vee
is in the kitchen."

"I thought I heard her in here. I'm sorry," Matt said. His
voice had a formality, a control, that made it somehow

more an acknowledgment of Eileen's half-dressed state than a wolf whistle would have been.

"She *was* in here," Eileen said. "Marie got me a bit wet, and Vee brought me up here to change." Her heart threatened to explode through her chest wall, it was banging so, but she managed to keep her voice steady.

Time and the world stood still. Then Matt covered the distance between them with two fierce strides, and time and the world swirled in dizzying rhythms.

"Little one," he breathed, he chanted. His hands grappled at her shoulders, as though searching for the impressions he might have carved when he touched her skin before. "You're more than beautiful. More than desirable. You're desire itself, damn you. I must have you. I will have you."

"Matt," she began, but his mouth was on her mouth, his lips owned her lips, his breath owned her words. They stood locked in a soundless embrace, propping each other up against the downward pull of the Earth.

They came up for air. Matt put his hands in Eileen's hair. He ruffled the short, dark strands. "When I saw your hair, when I realized what I was seeing—" He shook his head in wonder. "Marvelous!" he intoned. "You did go to the Chandelier that night, didn't you? You had your hair cut for me, and then you kept our date—a little late, but you kept it?"

"You mean you were there?" She told her jubilant heart to take it easy. What if disappointment lurked? But she couldn't check the words.

"Of course I was there, my silly one, my darling. Do you think I searched the world for someone like you, only to let you go like that? It took all the self-discipline I had not to follow you from the Clemence that morning, not to ask your name or where you were staying. I had to know that you cared, though. I had to risk losing you forever to know that. Because to have you without knowing that—" He shrugged. "That would be worth nothing."

Suddenly Eileen felt another rising wave of the outrage

this man kept provoking in her. "Your feelings were that intense—and yet you couldn't wait twenty minutes for me?"

"You don't understand."

Angrily she turned away and plucked a pair of Vee's jeans off the pile. She thrust one leg and then the other into the faded denim pants. "Oh, I understand. You have an ego bigger than Mont Blanc. And a faithfulness quotient as small as Le Salève. Did you call your blond friend," making the word as scathing as she could manage, "to console yourself that night? Or was it someone else?" She zipped up the pants. They were two inches too big at the waist. She looked hopelessly around.

"Sorry I'm not wearing a tie," Matt said, in the maddeningly casual voice she remembered so well. "Will this do?" He took a large, square, bandana-patterned handkerchief from the back pocket of his corduroy pants. "I think if you fold this up along the diagonal, it will just make it around that slender waist. My God, you're beautiful when you're angry. Corny, I know, but it's true. Promise me you'll never ever grow your hair again."

"Oh, do shut up about my hair!" Eileen hurled at him. To her horror, tears welled up in her eyes. "You didn't even notice it last night at the Richemond, did you? All you could see was your blonde and maybe your reflection in her eyes. You, the great observer, the visual hotshot." She balled up his handkerchief and hurled it at him. "I have a scarf in my bag. Downstairs. I don't need any help from you. Who knows what waist that scarf was around last night?"

"Little one. Eileen."

"Don't ever call me 'little one' again." She stormed out of the room. She hurried along the hallway. From below she could hear the rise and fall of conversation. She wasn't ready to face Vee and Pierre and Alan just yet, and she kept walking until she found the room she wanted.

"Hi! More pouch!" a small voice called out.

"Hello, sweetheart. I think you're supposed to be going

to sleep now, aren't you? What a pretty crib. I like those lambs."

"No crib. Want down."

"Oh, I'll get into all sorts of trouble if I take you down. What if I tuck you in and tell you the pouch story again? Will that do?"

"More pouch!" Marie agreed happily, and hunkered down under her pink satin coverlet.

Twice through the story and Marie was asleep. Eileen lingered a while in the nursery, inhaling the vibrations of utter peacefulness that issue from a sleeping child, then she went downstairs.

"Hello!" Vee called out. "We thought you'd gotten lost."

"I couldn't resist a detour by the nursery. Your famous nonsleeper has conked out beautifully." Eileen crossed the room, opened her leather pouch, pulled out a silk flower-print scarf, and ran it through the loops of Vee's jeans.

"Gorgeous," Alan declared. "You'll start a new rage."

Pierre stood up. "I don't know about our guests, but I'm getting hungry. Shall I get the oil bubbling, *cherie*?" He turned to Eileen and Alan and explained, "We're having fondue bourguignonne tonight—a slightly inauthentic but very delicious affair. We put a pot of simmering grape-seed oil in the middle of the table, then each of us spears pieces of raw tenderloin and cooks it in the oil for a minute, and *voilà*!"

"That sounds wonderful," Eileen enthused, though her stomach was still churning from her encounter upstairs with Matt. She looked around the room. Where was her tormentor, anyway?

Pierre vocalized the question she was thinking. Vee shrugged casually, but Eileen thought she glimpsed real worry in the stewardess's eyes.

"He may have gone out to his studio," Vee said, explaining to Alan and Eileen that they had an unused woodshed behind the house where Matt kept an easel and a set of oils and brushes.

"Well, that's that," Pierre declared, none too happily. "He could be all night. Let's go ahead and have dinner without him." He shook his head. "I'm very fond of that brother of yours, Vee, but sometimes he acts like an overgrown adolescent. We have dinner guests. I don't care what he's feeling, he should pull himself together and participate in the evening."

"Maybe there's a *foehn* blowing up," Eileen suggested, and the others laughed. Swiss folklore held that when a certain wind—the *foehn*—was blowing, people behaved irrationally. "The guidebook said you could even get away with murdering your wife during the *foehn*. Is that true?" she asked, shivering a little.

"Nonsense," Vee stated firmly. "Anyway, this isn't *foehn* weather. It's crisp and cold out, not warm and wet. No, what's wrong with Matt has nothing to do with the weather." She gave Eileen a long, slow look with a hint of a knowing smile, and Eileen knew that her give-away cheeks were flooding with color. "We'll discuss this later," Vee told her husband. "Meanwhile, let's eat. I'm starved."

Despite the tension she was feeling, Eileen's appetite was spurred by the delicious smells and amusing ritual of fondue bourguignonne. Each diner was given not only a mound of thinly sliced beef to cook in the bubbling oil but a selection of sauces as well, varying from a delicate concoction that tasted of whipped cream and mustard to a pungent vinegar-based puddle with capers floating in it.

Halfway through the meal Eileen's fork collided with another in the cooking pot, and the meat fell from her prongs. Pierre immediately announced with glee that Eileen had to pay the traditional forfeit—a kiss for every man at the table. She quickly got up and dropped an affectionate buss on Pierre's high-domed forehead and a soft peck on Alan's cheek. She tried not altogether successfully to keep from imagining the sort of kiss she would have bestowed on Matt if he'd been present at the table.

Several times she stole glances at the chair where he would have sat. Even in his absence, he was more there

for her than the people who were really and actually there.
She loved him. She hated him.

The fondue bourguignonne was primarily Pierre's doing.
Vee contributed the crisp salad of ruby-leaf lettuce, water-
cress, and endive, and the crusty home-baked bread (not
the least bit burned) and an array of room-temperature
cheeses. Dessert, Vee immodestly announced as she brought
it to the table, was a joint effort—probably her and Pierre's
finest collaboration since Marie. It was a Mont Blanc, a
mountain of shaved chestnut sluiced with vanilla-flavored
whipped cream. No one at the table had to be told that the
heavenly rich sweet derived its name from its visual resem-
blance to a certain important mountain.

Conversation over dessert quite naturally turned to the
Mont Blanc Watch Company, particularly to its rather intriguing president, Jean-Claude Longemalle of the many
marriages.

"Each wife younger than the one before," Vee declared.
"Régine can't be more than twenty-five." It occurred to
Eileen that her redheaded friend had a unique ability to
gossip without sounding malicious.

"Does he have children?" Eileen asked. She felt that she
really wanted to get a handle on the man, and this was the
place to get it.

"No kids," Vee answered. "Rather sad, isn't it? He's made
that company what it is, and he has no real heirs to leave
it to."

"Now that I think about it," Eileen commented, "the two
men we met in his office were rather like a pair of com-
petitive sons each trying to win the old man's favor. Don't
you think so, Alan?"

Alan nodded. "Exactly, baby. And I'm just afraid we're
going to be middled in there. Unless you come up with a
catch phrase so superb that neither of his boys can argue
against it."

Eileen picked up her wine glass. The deliciously thin
white wine they'd been drinking before dinner had been
superseded by a full-bodied red to accompany the fondue

bourguignonne, which in turn had given way to an extra, extra dry champagne with dessert. She took a small sip of the bubbly. It prickled pleasingly. "Maybe I'm just getting drunk," she said, "but I think I'm getting closer. It's funny, I feel more like a psychologist right now than a would-be copy writer. If I can just understand Jean-Claude Longemalle, I think that right phrase will come popping out."

She leaned back in her chair. She drank in the rich, chocolate tones of the room. Matt's paintings were—like his personal presence—noticeably missing. The dark brown paneling on the walls was interrupted here and there by wallpapered sections depicting hunting scenes. There was no hanging art.

"Tell me more," she prompted Vee. "He's building a new house?"

"He claims his wife insisted on it—that she didn't want to live where her predecessors lived. But Matt says that Longemalle is deeply involved in the house himself. Matt had a curious comment the other day, in fact. He said every time he thought he'd arrived at a final blueprint, Longemalle came up with some big change. A new wing here. Another story there. It's almost as though, Matt said, Longemalle wants to prolong the building process as much as possible, as though he dreads the day when its completed."

"Of course!" Eileen sat bolt upright. Clarity flooded into her mind, sweeping away the muzziness wrought by drink. "The young wife, the pretend sons, the house that he doesn't want finished because he doesn't want it to be his mausoleum—don't you see? He's buying time." She turned to Alan. His eyes were glowing.

"Buy a Mont Blanc watch," Eileen phrased slowly, looking around the table. "Buy time."

"Baby!" Alan exclaimed. "I think you've done it! He was worried about selling to inflation-troubled Americans, but if there's a better hedge against inflation than buying gold and silver, it's buying time. Fantastic! You're a genius!"

"I don't know anything about the advertising game,"

Pierre commented from the other end of the table, "but it sounds pretty solid to me."

"Oh, Eileen, I can see it on the pages of the best magazines, I can see it on billboards," Vee cried. "And to think you thought of it here. I'm sure he'll love it."

"Buy time," Eileen repeated happily. "That is pretty good, isn't it?"

"It's brilliant," drawled a familiar deep voice behind her. "You've got the old boy's psyche pegged perfectly. You'll probably sell a million watches for him." Then, as Eileen turned to look at him, Matt shook his head as if in sorrow and said, "That's what living in New York does to you. What a waste of an intelligent mind."

chapter 11

EILEEN FINESSED THE promised ride back to Geneva with Matt. She and Alan would take the train, she insisted to Vee, never mind that at this hour the trains were molasses-slow. Vee didn't press the issue. Even a much less perceptive woman than Vee would have realized that an enormous tension existed between Matt and Eileen.

As the train chugged along the Lake, and her wine-and-champagne high wore off, Eileen began to succumb to a sense of loss. Vee and Pierre and little Marie had engendered a wave of family sentiment in her. Vee might have been the sister she never had and always wanted, and what more rewarding niece than Marie?

Yet she would not be seeing them again, she determined. She was going to steer clear of everyone and everything remotely linked with Matt Edwards.

"Hey, baby; hey, pal; what's the matter?" Alan kept prodding. "You should be all up. I know that Longemalle will love your idea. You're going to be a hero around the Marsden Agancy. You want to be a copy writer? I bet the job is yours for the asking now."

She evaded his friendly questions. "I'm just tired, Alan. And I had an awful lot to drink. I've been a bit of a lush since I came to Geneva. I think maybe it's time I went back to Coca-Cola."

"You're cute when you drink," Alan told her. "Anyway, you make a couple of glasses of wine sound like half a bottle of whiskey. You won't even have a headache in the morning, I bet. You've probably never had a hangover in your whole life, have you?"

"Not a real one, I don't suppose. Have I missed something wonderful?"

Alan put his hand on her arm. Night hurtled by outside the window. "Oh, I do like you, Eileen Connor," he said. "I like your spirit."

"I like you, too, Alan."

"I mean I *like* you," he repeated, with stronger emphasis.

She shook her head, trying to forestall further conversation along these lines, but he clearly was not to be deterred from saying his piece.

"I have to admit that character was never the number-one thing I looked for in women," he told her, "but now that I've seen it, I'm not sure how I'm going to like women who don't have it. The way you handled that creep who kept trying to put you down tonight—"

"Please. Please don't, Alan."

"You were sensational," he went on heedlessly. "You somehow managed to deliver a couple of real good karate chops without ever stopping being a lady."

"Alan, I beg you, don't say anymore."

Alan ran nervous fingers through his straight blond hair. "You're not mad at me, are you? Do you think I should have come to your rescue more tonight? Should I just have punched the guy out?"

"Alan, you're making me desperate!" Eileen finally cried. "Don't you understand?"

"Understand what, baby?"

"I'm in love with that man—that creep, as you call him. He's the worst thing that's happened to me since my ex-husband, maybe since forever, and I'm in love with him. I'm in love with him and I never want to see him again and I would be extremely grateful if you would stop talking about him, if in fact you would stop talking period!" She flung herself as far away from him as the geography of their adjoining train seats would permit, and for a few moments there was no sound in the half-empty car except for the spinning and grinding of the wheels.

Then Eileen unwrapped herself and peeked at Alan. He

was staring straight ahead. "I'm sorry," she told him, her voice as small as a girl's now. "I like you, and I'm sorry I lost my temper."

"It's okay, baby." Alan's mouth relaxed into something like a smile. "I understand. I guess we're both sort of in the same boat, aren't we?"

"What do you mean?"

"We're both in love with someone we can't have."

Eileen shook her head furiously. She couldn't bear the notion that Alan was putting his feelings for her into the same category as hers for Matt Edwards. Alan liked her for real, she knew, and maybe admired her, and very probably wanted to sleep with her, and quite possibly would have been happy to be an "item" with her for a while, to use the current office parlance; but what did those feelings have to do with the great tumult of emotions she experienced at the very thought of her tall stranger? What Alan felt for her he'd felt for other women and would feel again. What she felt for Matt was a once-in-a-lifetime event. Not even Keith had stirred her so.

No. There was no comparison. Maybe it was arrogance on her part to decide that, but she was sure she was right. It wasn't that she was judging Alan less capable than she of feeling violent passion. She just couldn't believe that that was what he felt for her. He was just too—normal around her. And she'd seen him in heat before, back in New York, mooning around one of the other secretaries or maybe a glamorous client. Definitely no comparison.

Besides, she could have Matt Edwards if she wanted him. There was no need to tell Alan this, no need to crush his ego altogether, but she could certainly have Matt. His lips, his eyes had offered themselves up utterly. His body was hers to shudder beneath. His sweat was hers to taste.

If she didn't mind sharing him with a certain blonde and probably a dozen other blondes and maybe some brunettes too.

He was hers to have, if a moment was enough.

She laughed softly.

"What?" Alan asked.

She shook her head. "Nothing," she said. She couldn't tell him that she'd been mentally rehearsing the delicious moment when Matt would call her and say he wanted to see her—and she would turn him down. Every cell in her body and being longed to be bonded to his, but she would not give in to that longing. Better to pass through this lifetime without ever knowing the supreme pleasure of being one with her true love than to have that oneness be, for him, just another pleasurable passage.

"You're lucky, you know," she remarked to Alan after a while.

"How's that?" He held himself a little stiffly. His voice lacked its usual jauntiness.

"Not being plagued by jealousy and possessiveness."

"Like I told you, I would probably be devilishly jealous if I cared enough. I'd be damned possessive of you," he added, "if I possessed you in the first place."

He turned away, ineffably wistful, and a spasm of guilt shook Eileen. She was being brutally selfish, unforgivably insensitive. "Alan," she began softly, "would it do any good if I told you I was all wrong for you?"

"When in the whole history of bruised hearts did that ever do any good?" he returned, with a touch of his old tone.

"Probably I'm the first woman you ever got to know as a person," Eileen said. "Maybe if you had to work on a difficult project with every woman you fancied, instead of starting off by pursuing her to her bedroom, you'd have these feelings more often."

She held her breath, wondering if he'd resent her words, but he gave her his big boyish grin and said lightly, "You've probably got something there, Doctor. I'll think it over. Meanwhile, I promise you, I'll do my best not to assault you with my intentions—honorable or otherwise."

"Do you want to hear a terrible confession?" Eileen asked.

"The more terrible the better."

"In a way I'll be relieved if you stop flirting, but in a way I'll probably miss it. I mean, I'll start wondering if it's time for another haircut or should I change my perfume or something."

"Baby, you are the damnedest creature I've ever encountered. Breathtakingly honest, and utterly impossible. Whatever am I supposed to do about you? I think my father was right. You can't live without women, he always said, but you can't live with them."

"Funnily enough, that's what my mother always said about men," Eileen giggled.

They shook their heads in unison, vowed deep "palship" unto the ages, and rode on toward Geneva in pleasant silence.

chapter 12

EILEEN WOKE TO the first cloudy sky she'd seen since her arrival in Switzerland. The room-service waiter who brought breakfast told her that snow was expected later in the day. He sounded as excited as a small boy and Eileen knew why from her guidebook; although the mountains surrounding Geneva were snow-capped much of the year, the city itself was rarely dusted with the white stuff. Eileen was excited too. She'd always loved weather. She wouldn't even have minded, she thought, submitting herself to the ill-reputed *foehn*. One of the complaints she had about New York life was that most of the inhabitants grumbled about anything but mild temperatures and clear skies.

Predictably, Alan Scott was displeased at the prospect of a storm.

"It'll be so beautiful, though," Eileen said. "I bet the snow here is a hundred times whiter than in New York."

Alan picked absently at the remains of one of Eileen's breakfast *croissants*. "It'll gum everything up," he complained. "It always does."

"Don't be silly. They're only expecting an inch or so."

"I wonder what's doing back in New York?" Alan walked over to the window and craned his neck, as though trying to see beyond the Lake and the mountains to the far side of the Atlantic.

"Nice mushy slush, I bet. Don't tell me you're homesick, Alan."

"Just in a rotten mood," he replied. The instant the words were out, his mood seemed to lighten a little, at least enough to let him make jokes. "And how are you today, my beautiful tormentress?"

"Terrific." she exclaimed, with Madison Avenue bravura. Then she laughed. "Hanging in there." She looked at the battered traveling alarm clock on her bedside table. "I suppose someone's in at Mont Blanc by now. Shall I call and get us an appointment with the Terrible Threesome? Do you still like my slogan enough to go to them with it?"

"Do I like it! Baby, it's about all I have in the world right now. Sure, I like it. I love it. I love you, and I love it, and I'll thank you not to look at me as if I were a close cousin of the Cookie Monster." He nervously smoothed back his straight fair hair. "Call them. Line it up. I'm supposed to check in with Marsden at ten A.M. New York time, and I'd like to have something wonderful to tell them all, so see if Longemalle won't meet with us this morning or early afternoon."

Eileen went to the telephone and, in French that was flowing more and more naturally off her tongue every day, negotiated with two secretaries at Mont Blanc. Finally she reported back to Alan that Longemalle was spending the morning showing a group of international diplomats around the factory, had a lunch appointment with a famous designer of women's clothing, and wouldn't be able to see the American advertising team until three o'clock. Ernst Vogt and Roger St. Denis would be available earlier, however, if Alan wanted a preliminary meeting.

He shook his head. "I don't trust those two. Besides, Longemalle is the one you've really keyed your thinking to, and Longemalle is the one who has to make the final decision anyway."

Eileen said she quite agreed, impatient though she was to sound out her ideas with anyone at Mont Blanc. Then, "What shall we do with the morning?"

Alan looked meaningfully in the direction of her bed.

"Oh, Alan, cut it out. I thought you were going to be good."

"And I thought you were going to get nervous if I was *too* good."

"Yes, well, don't worry about it. I mean, you'll probably be bad enough even if you don't try to be bad. Anyway, to blatantly change the subject, I have a couple of errands to do. I'd like to send some kind of bread-and-butter present to Vee and Pierre. Maybe a present for Marie would be what they'd appreciate the most."

"That's a good idea. Can't we get that together? It ought to come from me too, don't you think?"

"Sure. That would be nice. But you don't have to go shopping with me. I can put both our names on the card."

Alan said, "I get the feeling you wouldn't mind spending the morning on your own." He sighed. "Maybe I'll go work out my frustrations on the tennis court. Is our connection at Le Club Tennis still good? Do you think you can get me court time this morning?"

"Yes, sir. Coming right up, sir. What are you going to do about a partner?"

"Oh, you know how these clubs work. There's always a snazzy blonde who's just had a serving lesson with the pro and can't wait to show her stuff to some stranger." He looked eagerly at Eileen. "Did that get you just a teeny, tiny bit jealous?"

"Can't you see? I'm turning eleventy-seven shades of green," Eileen drawled. Then impulsively she hugged her colleague. "I hope you play with a fifty-year-old man with a double chin."

"That, *mademoiselle*, is the nicest lie anyone's ever told me. Want to rendezvous for lunch? We still haven't had a proper cheese fondue."

"Let's see when I can get you a court. Then we'll figure it out from there." She made a quick phone call and told him he had a court at ten-thirty. They agreed to meet back at the hotel at one. They would go for fondue and then head to Mont Blanc to keep their appointment with Longemalle and his cohorts.

Eileen strolled out into the cloudy day. For a while she wandered aimlessly along the quay bordering the Lake. The water today had an angry chop and a faint hint of green that reminded her of one of Matt Edwards's paintings hanging on the walls of his sister's house. She shook her head with an angry chop of her own. Could she do nothing in the world without running the risk of conjuring the image of that man?

She forced herself away from the water and her own thoughts into an ultra-modern department store. She quickly found the toy department and almost immediately set eyes on the perfect present for little Marie. It was a three-foot-high stuffed kangaroo, its fur a lovely burnished carmel color, with a pouch big enough to hold a tot's pajamas. "Ouch. My pouch! Not a couch!" Eileen wrote on a gift card and signed it, "with love and kisses from your American friends, Alan and Eileen." The sales clerk assured her with just a touch of sniffiness that the Swiss Postal Service would have no trouble at all conveying the parcel to Vevey by the next morning.

The department store had a candy counter of rather staggering proportions, and Eileen decided to send some presents back to the United States. For her parents she chose a big box of nut-and-fruit filled chocolates, the box adorned with a brilliant photograph of Lake Geneva and the surrounding mountains. She sent smaller assortments to several of the other secretaries at the Marsden Agency.

As she wrote out the New York address, she panged. New York seemed very far away—and not unpleasantly so. For all that she'd praised the architecture of the city to Matt Edwards, she felt no great urge to return to the shrill hustle of Madison Avenue and the unnatural stillness of her own small apartment. And, as she visualized her sister secretaries sitting at their desks, she visualized herself returning to her pre-Geneva work routine: regular hours, predictable tasks, and a distinct absence of sparkling lakes and fresh-baked *croissants*.

And a distinct absence of tall strangers.

She knew a little bit about herself, about human nature. She knew that she'd recovered from the loss of Keith, although once she would have deemed recovery impossible. Getting on the plane for Geneva, talking with Vee, wallowing for a last time in her misery, and finally meeting Matt Edwards: These factors had helped to heal her.

And someday, back in New York, she would recover from her agonizing, conflicting feelings about the stranger, about Matt. The hitch, the terrible hitch, was that the very thought of recovering from him seemed a kind of obscenity, an insult to life. She knew she would recover nonetheless; she knew she might even fall in love again. The psyche was like that. One healed. And one died a little.

She might even marry. She might end up in the kind of classic suburban existence Alan Scott and she had been talking about on the train—a house in Westchester County, a station wagon, and 2.4 kids. She would love those children very much. But every once in a while an angry stretch of water or another man's profile or a sardonic laugh or a cobblestone street would bring Matt to mind, and she would feel her soul shrink another millimeter.

She looked for a clock. None in sight. Funny to be in Switzerland and not instantly know the hour. Finally she asked the clerk behind the candy counter and learned: a few minutes before noon.

She started back for her hotel. She wasn't due to meet Alan for nearly an hour; she was already dressed for lunch and the meeting at the Mont Blanc Watch Company. She had quite another reason for returning to the Richemond.

By now there would be a message from Matt, she was sure of it. Wanting to see her. To hold her, to bruise her arms, to devour her lips, to possess her . . .

The night before she'd made up her mind that she would not see him. Surely she longed to be his lover as intensely as he longed to be hers. His words echoed in her mind: "I must have you. I will have you." And her own voice matched it and drowned it out: *Yes*.

But there was an enormous, vital difference between

them. That difference was symbolized in Eileen's mind by a blue chiffon scarf. Matt wanted her because he wanted women. Vee's statements about her brother and the evidence in front of Eileen's eyes made that the inescapable conclusion. And she wanted Matt because she'd never wanted anyone else. He was the man from her dream of the cave; she knew that now with a feverish certainty. She'd only married Keith because she'd given up believing that such a man really existed.

An enormous, a vital, an insuperable difference. Better to turn her back on his desire and her own than to have what she most craved in all the world and have it tainted. That's what she'd decided the night before.

Yet now, as she walked along beneath the gathering clouds, she wondered if she'd made the right decision. Never to see him again, never to rage at him again, never to feel his fingers branding their shape into her shoulders: madness. Maybe she should see him just once more. Kiss him just once more.

"I have to buy time," she said aloud, and laughed at the coincidence, the irony.

She began to quicken her pace. Shoulders high, a smile on her elfin face, she walked into the Hotel Richemond and crossed the lobby.

"I'd like my messages," she told the desk clerk. "*Mademoiselle* Connor, room six twenty-eight."

The clerk looked in box 628. He checked with the hotel telephone operator. He looked in box 628 again. He shook his head.

No messages for *Mademoiselle* Connor. Not a one.

chapter 13

JEAN-CLAUDE LONGEMALLE had only one word to say in response to Eileen's idea: "*Brava!*" He rose from his seat at the head of the conference table and kissed Eileen's hand. Eileen could almost feel the wave of relief and jubilation washing over Alan's being.

She'd done it. She'd come through. Longemalle was crazy about the slogan "Buy time." Predictably, his sycophant employees mirrored his enthusiasm; in fact, Roger St. Denis and Ernst Vogt outdid themselves praising the slogan once they saw that praise was what Longemalle wanted. Longemalle was once again fired up about the notion of selling his watches in the United States. Marsden had the account. Eileen had saved the day.

"'Buy time.' It is so very profound," Longemalle rhapsodized. "People will realize we are not merely offering them a product, we are offering them an eternal verity."

"And at the moment when everyone is so worried about the devaluation of the dollar, what more comforting thought than the notion that the most precious commodity on earth is still theirs to purchase?" Ernst Vogt's words were an elaboration of the theme that Alan had postulated at Vee's and Pierre's house.

"I think," Roger St. Denis chimed in, "that we might even want to use the slogan for our own local advertising, if Marsden would permit. *Achetez du temps*—yes, I think it works very well in French."

"We'll need a few days to put together a real campaign," Alan said smoothly. "The agency may want to send a creative team over to work here with us, or they may want us to return to New York and do the work there, and then one of us would return with the presentation for your approval."

"I'm sure our approval will be readily forthcoming," Monsieur Longemalle said, "as long as *Mademoiselle* Connor is involved in your efforts."

"Of course. Of course. This is her baby. Wouldn't have it any other way."

"Good." With an imperious gesture, Longemalle dismissed Vogt and St. Denis. Then he said to Alan and Eileen, "We must celebrate this event. You must come have dinner at my home tonight. My wife is having one of her little parties. I think you will not be bored."

Eileen's brain whirred. "That's very kind of you," she began, "but I don't think—"

"I won't hear a word of it. It's not black tie, so you needn't worry about dress, if that's the question. And you won't be the only Americans. My wife and I have commissioned a very brilliant young American architect to do a house for us, and he'll be there. Quite the colorful character, he is." Eileen felt Alan stiffen next to her. Longemalle went on blithely, "And the skier Christophe Perot will be there, and several of our fine local musicians from the Swiss-Romande Orchestra—quite the bright young crowd. You'll feel right at home, I'm certain."

The fondue she'd eaten for lunch suddenly loomed heavy in Eileen's stomach. But she knew there was no out. She mustered her most gracious smile and told Monsieur Longemalle that the evening sounded delectable and of course they'd be honored to take part.

"Good. Seven o'clock, then. Let me write down the address for you. We're about a fifteen-minute ride from your hotel. Any taxi driver will know how to find us."

"Well, baby," Alan said, when they were out on the street, "looks like you get to spend another evening with your dreamboat."

"What a way to celebrate!" Eileen cried crossly.

"I thought you'd be thrilled to your toes. You said the man was the love of your life."

"That doesn't mean I want to see him." Not this way, at least, she added to herself.

"Women," Alan sighed theatrically.

A few soft snowflakes drifted down out of the now leaden sky. Eileen stuck out the tip of her tongue the way she'd always done as a child and tasted a flake or two. Delicious.

"I suppose the snow means we'll have trouble getting a taxi tonight," Alan observed gloomily.

"Come on. It's not a major blizzard blowing up, you know. Anyway, aren't you looking forward to the party? *You'll* probably have a good time."

"You think I'm looking forward to another encounter with The Stormy One? And having to watch you hang on to his every word?" They walked along in silence for a moment, then Alan added, "Hey, I'm not being totally honest with my pal. You know the woman I played tennis with this morning?"

"Sure." Eileen had heard a great deal over lunch about the partner Alan had lucked into at Le Club Tennis, the snazzy blonde with the smashing serve right out of his fantasies.

"Well, I was thinking about calling her up and trying to make a date for tonight."

"Aha, you rascal. It certainly didn't take you long to get over me. I'm almost jealous," she said, not totally untruthfully.

"Who said anything about being over you? Separate compartments, baby."

"Well, maybe you'll find another snazzy blonde at the party tonight," Eileen consoled him. "Or maybe *Madame* Longemalle will take a fancy to you. It's a pretty wide-open marriage, I guess, from the things Vee said."

"Your friendly old neighborhood womanizer draws the line at married women. If their husbands go along with their playing around, it's somehow even worse."

They walked the mile or so back to the Richemond. The rooftops of the city were so many gingerbread houses dusted with powdered sugar. Alan suggested that they stop off at the bar and have a drink to recover from their snowy trek and to celebrate their success with Jean-Claude Longemalle and company.

"I thought you had to call the office," Eileen said. "It must be just about time, if they're expecting to hear from you at ten o'clock New York time."

Alan looked at his watch. "You're right. The walk took longer than I realized. Will you place the call or should I?"

"Would you mind placing it? I want to stop at the desk for a moment. Then I'll be right up. Meet you in your room, okay?"

"Okay to that anytime," Alan grinned, and started toward the elevators.

Once again, her heart pounding, Eileen checked at the desk for messages. And this time: yes, indeed, a message for *Mademoiselle* Connor. She took the folded slip of paper from the desk clerk and thanked him in a tremulous voice.

She unfolded the message and read: "Please call Vee Lenke at 06-20-180."

Eileen put the piece of paper in her big brown leather shoulderbag. She felt a two-pronged wave of regret. It was sad that Matt hadn't called. And it was sad that she couldn't go upstairs and pick up the phone and dial Vee's number and hear her friend's bubbly tones. But at least with Vee there would be some kind of telephathic understanding, she was certain of it. Vee was too smart to mistake Eileen's failure to return her call for anything but what it was—a reflection of her torturous confusion over Matt.

Damn him! Why did she ever have to meet him? Why did she have to wake up?

She stood waiting for an elevator. She wondered if Alan had had any trouble placing the call. Sometimes the mechanics of life seemed to throw him. But all the hotel operators spoke English, among many other languages. Probably he'd managed fine.

She had to pass her room to get to Alan's. Just as she got to her door, she heard the telephone ring inside. She groped for her key, she found it, she got it into the lock, she opened the door. The ringing stopped.

"This is madness," she whispered. "I'm a prisoner."

She picked up the phone and got the hotel operator. Did the operator have any idea, she inquired, who'd just called room 628? The operator said she hadn't put through the call and would check with the other women at the switchboard. No messages, she reported back. Eileen felt ridiculous, but she couldn't stop her next question: Had the caller been a man or a woman? A man, the operator reported, a trifle impatiently. Eileen thanked her profusely and hung up.

She went into her bathroom and downed a glass of cold water. Finally composed enough to get on with life, she headed for Alan's room.

"I just hung up," he reported, as he let her in.

"Did you have any trouble getting through?"

"No, none."

His voice was strangely shaky, and Eileen looked at him curiously. "Is everything okay?"

"Oh, everything's terrific, baby. Old man Marsden was pleased as hell."

"What's going to happen now? Are they sending a creative team over?"

"Marsden made one of those world-famous thirty-second executive decisions of his. He said he was going to pull Kagan and Grimes off the Tidy Di-Dee account and have them work up a full-fledged presentation over the weekend, then they'll put it on a Swissair flight and we should have it Monday. Meanwhile you and I just sit tight and feel terrific about ourselves. Marsden said he figured it would cost him less to maintain us at the Richemond for a few extra days than to pay for airfare an extra time around. Provided we don't drink too much, he said. He could just send the presentation over cold, of course, but he figured that as long as we'd done the spade work with Longemalle, we'd better be on hand and deliver it up personally in case there are any problems."

"What did he think about the slogan itself? I was hoping that if he liked it enough he might want me to work on the copy for the ads."

Again Alan looked uneasy. His eyes didn't quite meet Eileen's. "He said, and I quote, '*Buy time* is probably the brightest bit of thinking to come from Madison Avenue since *Try it, you'll like it.*' But he thought with the tight schedule we have he'd better have the pros churn out the copy."

"Oh well," Eileen said philosophically, "I guess that's understandable. Maybe I'll get my chance back in New York. Alan, what on earth is wrong with you? You look terrible suddenly."

"I think maybe I'm coming down with something," Alan said. "Travel tummy."

"That fondue was pretty rich," Eileen agreed. "I've got some antacid in my room. Want me to get it for you?"

"No, I think I'll just stretch out for a while. Try to nap. I want to be in decent shape for Longemalle's party."

"Well, call me if you want anything. I might go for a little walk, then I'll be in my room. Gee, I better go make sure I didn't spot my red dress."

"You hardly had it on long enough to spot it," Alan said, referring to their aborted dinner date the night before last.

"It might need pressing, though. I'll call the valet. I hope they can do it this quickly."

"That's the sort of thing Swiss hotels are famous for." Alan looked out the window. The snow was coming down more heavily now. "You're really going to go for a walk in this stuff? Only you."

"Oh, not only me," Eileen murmured. She envisioned Matt Edwards in his rugged clothes. She was as sure as sure could be that he loved to walk in the snow. She looked over at Alan. He was quite alarmingly pale. "I do hope you'll be all right. Probably sleep would be the best thing. Do you want me to give you a call and wake you up?"

"I'll ask the hotel operator to ring me at five-forty-five. That'll give me an hour to shower and dress. I'll pick you up in your room at quarter of seven, okay?"

"Isn't that cutting things pretty close? I have a feeling that when you're invited for seven o'clock in Geneva, seven o'clock is what's meant. I don't think they believe in 'fashionably late.' And Longemalle did say it would be a fifteen-minute taxi ride."

"Okay," Alan agreed, "I'll pick you up at six-thirty." He kicked off his brown Bass loafers and stretched out on the bed. "Now be a good kid and let me get some sleep."

Eileen was still feeling a bit giddy over Marsden's enthusiastic response to her slogan. She chirped, "I never thought the day would come when you'd chase me out of a hotel room."

Alan smiled weakly and turned his back to her. Puzzled, almost hurt, she left his room.

chapter 14

THE SITUATION WAS too comical, too almost perfect in its irony, for Eileen to be upset. She, the notoriously tardy one, had been dressed, powdered, scented with Madame Rochas, and otherwise ready to go since six-fifteen. And here it was, twenty to seven, and there was no sign of Alan Scott. Amusing irony aside, the possibility loomed that they would be late for the Longemalles' party. She went to the telephone and asked the hotel operator to ring Alan's room.

From the groggy abruptness with which he answered, she realized to her distress that she'd woken him up. "Alan: What happened? Did the operator forget to call you?"

"Baby, sorry. No, I fell asleep before I could call the operator. What a lunkhead. You want to go ahead without me?"

"Don't be silly. But hurry. Can you meet me in the lobby in fifteen minutes? I'll have a taxi all revved up and raring to go."

"What a lunkhead," Alan repeated, seventeen minutes later, as their taxi headed through ever-thickening snow toward the Longemalle residence.

Eileen rather agreed, but she kept her agreement to herself. Alan still wore the slightly unstable air he'd manifested in the late afternoon, and she didn't want to ruffle him further. The invitation from Longemalle had had something of a royal command about it. She was afraid that if Longemalle took displeasure with her or Alan that evening, he was capable of withdrawing the Mont Blanc account from the Marsden Agency. Stranger things had happened. So:

best to bolster Alan's morale, not rip it down. He was more likely to charm if he felt good about himself.

"You look great," she tried for a starter. "Is that a new suit I glimpsed under your coat?"

"Nothing but," he said. "You wouldn't expect Alan Scott to go to London and not go shopping on Savile Row, would you?"

"Of course not, now that you mention it. You look like you're feeling better, too. Your stomach's okay?"

"Fine." He patted her gloved hand. "You're a lovely person, you are. Looking terrific yourself, by the way, as I don't have to tell you."

"It's always nice to hear." In fact, she was feeling un-usually self-confident. She had indulged in some French cosmetics on sale in a shop off the hotel lobby: a smoky gray eye shadow that she'd smudged along her lower lid, and a lip gloss called Wild, Wild Strawberry that perfectly matched one of the reds in her halter-necked dress.

She'd make Matt want her so badly that he'd think he couldn't live without her. And then— And then—

And then what? That was the part she kept backing and forthing about in her mind. Then what? She shuddered in ecstasy and pain.

"Some weather, eh?" the taxi driver commented in En-glish from the front seat. He was driving very slowly now. Eileen resisted the temptation to ask him the time.

"I thought we were only due for an inch or so," she said to him.

"What do they know?" The driver gave a Gallic shrug visible from the back seat. "My grandmother knows more about the weather from sticking her thumb out the window than these forecasters can tell you with their instruments and charts."

Alan rubbed a spot clear on the frosty window next to him. He peered out into the stormy night. "Where are we, anyway?"

"Near the Lake," Eileen answered. "The Palace of Na-tions is up that way."

"Not a bad life, living right on the Lake. The people here probably have their own docks and everything, you think?"

The taxi driver tooted angrily at a sports car that sped by and splashed the windshield with snowy slush. "You see that house there?" he asked. "The white one? It is said to belong to one of your Rockefellers. Their cozy little vacation cottage." He laughed. The house stretched this way and that, as big as a good-size hotel. "They have their own docks, they have a helicopter pad. Not bad, eh? And here we are *chez* Longemalle." He turned into a circular driveway. A vast turreted stone structure loomed beyond.

"Who could improve on this?" Alan asked, as they got out under the protective roof of a porte-cochère. "Your architect friend may be a world-class designer, but he's going to have trouble giving *Madame* Longemalle a house grander than what she's got."

"Maybe she wants something a little *less* grand," Eileen returned. "I think I'd get to feeling like Rapunzel if I lived with all these turrets. I'd want to move somewhere I could let down my hair."

A butler pulled open the heavy oak door as they approached it. Eileen wondered if some discreet electronic signal had announced their arrival. Certainly the precision engineering the Swiss watchmakers were renowned for could have spawned such a device. The butler's deference had more to do with ancient traditions of gracious service than with modern engineering, however. He even greeted Alan and Eileen by name, an impressive gesture from someone who had never seen them before.

He relieved Alan of his coat and directed Eileen to a small room off the entrance foyer, where a maid took her coat and offered the use of the best-equipped dressing table Eileen had ever seen. Not only did the table boast a remarkable array of cosmetics, combs, brushes, and scents in cut-glass bottles; it afforded Eileen a glimpse of herself in a three-sided mirror decked about with theatrical dressing room lights. Eileen dabbed a smidgen of powder on her nose and ran her fingers through her feathery hair to mess it up just so. Then she rejoined Alan in the foyer.

As the butler led them down a sconce-lit passageway, Eileen heard the unmistakable strains of a live string quartet. Monsieur Longemalle had mentioned that several members of the world-renowned Swiss-Romande Orchestra were going to be guests at the party; he had modestly failed to mention that the guests would be performing. They were playing a Beethoven quartet that was a great favorite of Eileen's parents and that, on record, had accompanied the family to Air Force bases the world over in Eileen's childhood. Eileen's spirit danced in rhythm with the passionate music. She felt equal to anything.

Then she realized, to her great dismay, as the butler opened a pair of double doors, that the quartet weren't, as she'd supposed, playing in an informal setting. They were arrayed on a proper little stage; and the Longemalles' guests were seated in gilded chairs set out in formal rows. As several heads turned, and the Longemalles rose from their separate seats to greet them, Eileen knew that their lateness was a real faux-pas. Why couldn't *Monsieur* Longemalle have told them that seven o'clock was curtain time? But of course he had supposed that they would be on time. One just was in Switzerland.

He greeted them warmly enough, but Eileen detected considerable reserve on the part of the elegant, tall, swan-necked, bosomy blonde who was the fifth *Madame* Longemalle. Eileen tried to apologize. Régine Longemalle simply cut off her words and ushered her and Alan into the last row of seats. Then, her emeralds jiggling in her deep de-colletage, she returned to her seat.

Her seat next to Matt Edwards.

On whose thigh she placed her ring-covered hand.

As the strains of Beethoven soared and swooped around her, Eileen wanted to die. She hadn't fallen in love with just another womanizer, she'd fallen in love with the play-boy of the Western world. Eileen felt a wave of real disgust. Had the man no standards? Here was Régine Longemalle, dripping jewels that were doubtless loving presents from her no-longer-young husband, and virtually under that husband's nose she was making obvious her feelings for a much younger, far handsomer man. This was the woman Matt Edwards liked tonight. Who would it be tomorrow—an out-and-out courtesan? In fact, an out-and-out courtesan would be a more honorable choice of playmate than Régine Longemalle.

Then why wasn't she cured? Eileen wondered frantically. Why did she still desperately long for Matt to turn around and move his lips in greeting? Why did she want him to look her up and down in her red dress and tell her again that she was desire itself?

"Are you okay?" Alan whispered from the next seat.

She started violently. "What?"

"The way you keep balling your fists—"

Eileen looked down at her tightly fisted hands. Slowly she unclenched them. Her nails had left indentations in her palms, twin sets of four little angry marks the shape of new moons. "Beethoven," she whispered. "I always get very emotional."

Though Alan looked unconvinced, he let the subject drop. Eileen tried to fix her eyes on the four musicians, her ears on the glorious sounds emanating from them. But her eyes kept straying to the back of Matt's dark head; her ears kept straining to pick up the occasional whispered word that passed between Matt and Régine.

The music ended. The audience of twenty or thirty applauded loudly.

"Is that it?" Alan asked Eileen.

"I guess so. People are getting up. Did you like the music?"

"Well, it's not my sort of thing, frankly, but they sure put a lot of energy into it. Did you like it?"

"I loved it," Eileen said.

"Even though it tortured you?"

"Sometimes you love what tortures you." Eileen stood up. "Let's go," she added. She wanted to get through the doorway before Matt and Régine passed the row where she and Alan were sitting.

They followed the crowd into a high-ceilinged room dominated by a buffet table worthy of a royal wedding reception.

"This sure beats a quick sandwich at your desk," Alan murmured, eying the mounds of iced oysters, the platters of crayfish, an array of coarse and smooth pâtés, what appeared to be a whole roast tenderloin of beef, and brilliant platters of fresh whole fruits and vegetables. "Are those white asparagus I see? Wow. Shall we head for it? Good thing my stomach recovered."

"A drink is what I want," Eileen said. At that moment the butler appeared with a trayful of brimming champagne glasses. She and Alan plucked glasses from it.

Jean-Claude Longemalle detached himself from a group of earnest-looking young men and, arms outstretched, approached Eileen and Alan. "I am so very glad to see you, my American friends," he cried warmly. He raised his own champagne glass and looked meaningfully at Eileen. "To my very brilliant and very beautiful business associate," he declared.

"Hear, hear," Alan chorused enthusiastically, and raised his glass to Eileen.

"I must introduce you to some of our other illustrious guests." He snared the cellist from the string quartet and performed introductions, then beckoned over a young woman in a sari whom he called the greatest poet to come out of modern India. To Eileen's vast dismay, he then shepherded her and Alan over to a small knot of people dominated by Matt Edwards and Régine Longemalle.

"Ah, the late Miss Connor," Matt incanted gravely, bowing. "I know her well." Régine Longemalle's flashing smile made evident her pleasure at his crack.

But Jean-Claude Longemalle did not appear pleased at all. He did not appear pleased with his wife's smile or with Matt's sardonic words. He instantly reached into one of the pockets of his impeccable navy pin-striped suit. He produced a woman's wrist watch, a platinum-encased oval of breathtaking thinness. He took Eileen's slender left arm and, as if it were the most everyday act in the world, clasped the watch around her wrist.

"Time must be a friend to such a good friend of time's," he declared. He kissed Eileen's hand. "No, please don't protest. It is only fitting that you wear a Mont Blanc watch. Consider it very small repayment for the very exceptional service you have rendered my company."

Eileen gaped at the magnificent watch. It was almost weightless on her wrist. Its face stared up at her with what, for a crazy instant, looked like friendliness.

"But—" she began.

"Please," *Monsieur* Longemalle interrupted. "Don't disappoint me by being conventional. If it makes things easier to explain to your mother, I will similarly decorate *Monsieur* Scott." He paused for a laugh and got it—except from his wife and Matt. Out of another pocket came a man's wrist watch, which he handed unceremoniously to Alan. Eileen translated Longemalle's remarks for her colleague.

She felt in an absolute quandary. She'd spent enough time around watches in the past few days to realize that the masterpiece which Longemalle had clasped around her wrist was the absolute top of the line and worth probably literally a hundred times as much as Alan's watch. She was deeply uneasy about accepting a present that valuable, about owning an artifact that valuable. Why, the insurance alone would probably cost more than she'd meant to spend on a watch. But she knew the watch was not worth relatively as much to Longemalle—that in a way it was as if she had come up with a slogan for the biggest manufacturer of Swiss chocolates and he had given her a bushel basket of bonbons. To refuse it might be to offend him deeply—even to lose the account for Marsden.

No, you're justifying, she told herself sternly. You simply can't accept that kind of present from a stranger.

Yet, to return it to him at once would be to undo a very satisfying turn of events—the look of undisguised dismay on Régine Longemalle's face, the look of raised-eyebrow astonishment on Matt's face.

She would keep it for now, she decided. And return it to *Monsieur* Longemalle the following day with a pretty little speech guaranteed to assure he took no offense.

She bestowed smiles all around. "The only problem I have with accepting this magnificent watch," she said to *Monsieur* Longemalle, "is that I will no longer have an excuse for being late. Thank you very, very much. I never hoped to own anything to spectacular." She looked at the walls. They were hung with French Impressionist paintings—the real thing, she was certain. "It's as if I suddenly had a Renoir or a Monet to wear on my wrist," she added. Alan echoed her profuse thanks, and she translated his remarks for Jean-Claude Longemalle.

The venerable company president looked exceedingly gratified. He called for more champagne all around.

Régine Longemalle turned to Eileen with a wide smile that was utterly devoid of warmth. "So," she said, in dramatically accented English, "you have given my husband a new lease on life. He has never gone to the United States, you know, though he has traveled to nearly every other part of the globe. I think it gives him great satisfaction to think that his precious watches will now be sold there. It's as if he himself were instantly going to be transplanted to New York, Chicago, San Francisco, Dallas. After all, he may not have time to visit each of those cities."

Eileen couldn't help gasping at the tall, bejeweled blonde's cruel reference to her husband's age. Jean-Claude himself showed no outward reaction. Matt's lips curled—in contempt, Eileen supposed, for a man who permitted his wife to humiliate him that way.

Jean-Claude Longemalle wasn't Eileen's favorite person in the world. She remembered with distaste the naked egotism he'd displayed in his first meeting with her and Alan. Still, she couldn't let Régine get away with her dig, particularly not since it seemed to have afforded Matt Edwards another dose of the wry amusement which his psyche apparently required at regular intervals.

"That's the trouble with being the sort of company president who concerns himself with every detail of running the
business," Eileen declared, as though she'd misunderstood
the other woman's statement about her husband. "But once
his watches are on sale in the United States, surely he will
want to give himself the pleasure of seeing them in the
windows of the finest shops on Fifth Avenue and elsewhere
in the country. After all, Jean-Claude Longemalle is the
man who has so much time he can *sell* it."

The round was clearly Eileen's, but Régine Longemalle
was not yet ready to give up the fight. She squeezed Matt's
arm and said, "Actually, I can think of one good reason to
visit the States, so I hope we do get to go." Then, with the
perfect timing of an accomplished actress, she added to
Matt, "I think I hear your stomach growling, you poor
thing. You must be starved. Come. Let me feed you. I'm
sure we'll find something edible over there." She flashed
her venomous smile again and led Matt away in the direction
of the buffet table.

To Eileen's great relief, several of the other guests
swooped down on Longemalle just then, and she and Alan
were able to escape. "That woman," she seethed.

"That sure was open warfare," Alan said. "She really
almost blew up when you made that crack about her
brother."

"Her brother?"

"What you said about Longemalle running the company
all on his own. Didn't you know that Roger St. Denis is
her brother?"

"I didn't know for a minute! Where did you pick that
up? How come he isn't here?"

"St. Denis mentioned it to me himself this afternoon. I
guess you were in a tête-à-tête with Longemalle. I don't
know why he isn't here. Vogt isn't either. Remember?
Longemalle sent them packing before he invited us? I suspect he just can't stand either one. But Dragon Lady probably makes him keep her brother on." Alan looked longingly

at the buffet table. "The coast is clear. Let's go dig in before all the asparagus goes."

Eileen followed him obediently. She was still a little worried about him. He was clearly in better shape than he'd been late that afternoon—maybe because of the champagne; but he wasn't really himself. She was pretty sure that something upsetting had transpired during his transatlantic phone conversation with Mr. Marsden. Hard to imagine what, though. Marsden should have been full of congratulations and nothing but.

As she heaped her plate with delicacies, she kept stealing looks at her left wrist. She'd always thought that a watch would be a burden and a nuisance, both physically and psychologically. But the Mont Blanc watch, with its almost unbelievable thinness, felt no weightier than a kiss on her wrist. It took the sting out of time itself. She remembered the woman back at the office who'd told her that perpetual lateness was a symptom of discontent. Maybe she'd outgrown that discontent.

She stole a look over at Matt. He was eating oysters with great gusto. Whatever it was he aroused in her, "discontent" was not the word for it. Rage, yes. Hatred, yes. Nothing as mild as discontent. Funny, though. She hadn't wanted to be late tonight. If Alan had put in his wake-up call, they wouldn't have been late. She'd known that Matt would be here, and she'd wanted to be exactly on time.

On time for a man she hated?

And loved.

Everything. Everything strong. All the violent emotions.

Suddenly she couldn't eat any more, not even another grape. She put her plate down on a side table. A maid immediately whisked it away.

"Can we go?" she asked Alan a few minutes later.

"What's the hurry? We don't have to work tomorrow."

"By the time we call a taxi and everything, though—"

"Maybe we can hitch a ride. See that blonde over there? The one with the halo of curls? I'm sure she has a sports car. Probably a Mercedes. You can just tell."

Eileen sighed. Blondes! She said to Alan, "You want an excuse to talk to her? Be my guest."

"You're a pal, pal." Alan ate the last asparagus on his plate, then set the plate down. He walked across the room in the direction of his fair target.

Eileen turned her back on the scene. She'd had enough of the man-woman business for the evening. She longed to get back to her hotel room and the novel she'd brought to read on the flight from New York and hadn't even begun. Sometimes it was much more agreeable to be immersed in fiction than in truth.

She turned her back and found herself facing Matt.

"Hello," he said. His voice was carefully neutral.

"Hello," she said.

"Has the faithful Alan deserted you?" he asked then, the old sardonic tone back in his voice. "It hardly seems possible."

"This evening is full of events that scarcely seem possible," Eileen retorted pointedly.

"Not to worry. He's probably only talking with that blonde to make you jealous. There's nothing to her, really. You don't have a thing to be nervous about."

"Oh, you checked her out, did you?" Eileen asked. "Of course. Blondes are your specialty. Where is your stewardess friend tonight? Flying off somewhere?"

She'd thrown daggers into the word "friend," but Matt seemed not to notice. "Helga Winter? No, she's flying to Hong Kong tomorrow with Vee. So you recognized her the other night, did you? She said you were rather giving her the hairy eyeball. Now, now. Mustn't hit."

"I wouldn't give you the satisfaction," Eileen muttered. "And where is our charming hostess? I'm amazed she's left you on your own this long. Or does she put me in the not-to-worry-about category? Tell me, Matt, won't it feel funny taking money from Jean-Claude Longemalle for designing his house? After everything else you've taken away from him?"

Just then the lights went out.

chapter 15

A WOMAN SCREAMED. Another woman giggled. There was the sound of a plate smashing to bits on the floor. *Monsieur* Longemalle's voice called for candles.

Eileen fought back a rising sense of panic. It's only the storm, she told herself. But she couldn't help feeling as though some awful evil presence had swooped down from the skies and blotted out goodness and light.

"Eileen? Darling?" Matt's voice, incredibly tender, all traces of sarcasm gone, fell on her ears like music. "Are you all right?" His arms found her and encircled her. His scent, his aura, filled the space around her.

"Matt. I—"

"Shhh, darling. Don't say a word. Not yet. Let's just steal the moment."

She let herself go limp against him. Around them confusion rose and feel in waves, but she didn't care. She didn't care about anything. Not about his wanderlust, not about his woman lust—not about anything. When the lights had gone off, reality had been suspended. They were back on stage again, snug in the confines of the drama called *Little One and the Tall Stranger*, controlled by a benevolent playwright, answerable to no one else—not even themselves.

She could hear his heart beating. She could feel the heat of his flesh. His body felt as solid and imposing as Mont Blanc. He was the all-knowing man from her dream of the cave.

No doubts. No fears.

Tears threatened. She blinked her eyes. The butler had set elaborate candelabra about the room and was lighting the candles one by one. The darkness turned to dimness. The play was over—or at least the act was. Reality obtained again.

Matt held her at arm's length. His eyes sought hers, found them, fixed them. Once again Eileen had the sensation—both terrifying and ultimately comforting—that he knew exactly what was on her mind.

"Trust your feelings," he whispered. "Can you do that? Your instincts are right, you know. Your compass is set at true north. But then there's that whole other layer in the way. All your notions. Trust yourself. Trust me. Can you do that yet?"

For a horrifying moment she slipped backward in time and her ex-husband, Keith, was saying: "Trust me. Trust me." At the time he'd said those words he'd been seeing his stewardess "friend" for two months.

She shook her head. "I was married," she blurted out. "He played around. He didn't want to leave me, at least not at first. He wanted to have me and the other women, too. I couldn't bear it." She ran her finger down the side of Matt's face, that beautiful lean face with the mysterious hollows. "I can't do it. Not even for you."

Matt gripped her shoulders so hard that she almost cried out. "You little fool," he cried passionately. "You little fool."

He turned abruptly and crossed the room to join Régine Longemalle.

chapter 16

ALAN'S FRIZZY BLOND new friend—a young English potter named Samantha—didn't have a Mercedes sports car, she had a dented old Volkswagen Beetle. In which unprepossessing vehicle she said she'd be glad to give Alan and Eileen a ride back to the Richemond, if she could get the car started.

The other departing guests were clustered in the foyer as members of the Longemalles' staff brought their cars under the porte-cochère. Samantha said her car was like a dog that only responded to its owner, and she would get it herself. Alan and Eileen trooped after her into the snowy night.

"Look." Alan pointed to a tree that had fallen, pulling wires with it. "I guess we know why the lights went out."

Samantha giggled. Eileen deduced that she and Alan had made the most of the sudden darkness. Oh, well, who was she to judge? she sternly lectured herself. She shook her head at her own folly.

Samantha got the car started as Alan offered nonstop advice and encouragement from the front passenger seat and Eileen huddled miserably in the back seat. As they inched their way toward the Richemond, Alan and Samantha hurled bright little sentences at each other. Eileen gathered that they'd both had rather a lot to drink. She hoped that Samantha was capable of driving. But what difference would it make if they all got killed? Great tears rolled down her cheeks.

"Hey, what's the matter, pal?" Alan called back brightly. "You're being awfully quiet."

Eileen surreptitiously wiped her eyes. "You young people just enjoy yourselves," she offered brightly. The attempt at witticism didn't quite come off.

"You're not sick or anything, are you?" Alan craned around to get a look at her. His voice definitely was slurring. "Wouldn't want anything t' happen t' my ace pal." He turned to Samantha, who was hunched in concentration over the wheel. "Eileen's the greatest. Yeah, the greatest." He told Samantha the whole story of the presentation that Longemalle hadn't liked—and Eileen's wonderful slogan that he'd loved.

"'Buy time,'" Samantha repeated. "Jolly good, that. Wouldn't it be lovely if we really could? I'd scrape and save like anything, and then splurge all my money on minutes and hours. And maybe if I were very, very good, dear old Santa would give me an entire extra day at Christmas. Oh, super. I guess you'll really be a hero back at the office, Eileen. Is there an advertising Hall of Fame on Madison Avenue? They'll put you in it for sure."

"She has her million-dollar watch," Alan said loudly. "Isn't that enough of a reward?"

"I'm not keeping the watch," Eileen said.

"You're not? But you said you were. Made a whole pretty speech. Least I guess it was pretty, since it was in French."

"I didn't want *Monsieur* Longemalle to lose face."

Alan chortled. "The watchmaker lose face. That's a good one."

"Is he always this beastly?" Samantha cheerily called back to Eileen.

"He's usually worse. Only kidding," she added hastily. "He's terrific. He really is. Three and a half stars. I recommend him highly."

"Hello," Samantha said. "Did you hear that?" She nudged Alan. "Can it be that for once I've fallen for a decent bloke? I have rather fallen for you, you know. Daddy packed me off to Geneva because last time around I fell for a not-at-all-nice bloke. Switzerland seemed the least likely place for him to look for me in. And there's a woman out at Veyrier, near Le Salève, who's a super potter, and I'd been wanting to work with her for some time." She managed to handle a small skid adroitly without so much as a pause for breath in her narrative.

"How did you meet the Longemalles?" Eileen asked, when she'd caught her own breath.

"Régine collects us artsy types for her salons. She's a bit much, isn't she? But I'll say this for her. She got the old man to start supporting the arts in a big way instead of letting all his money just molder away in the bank. She's kept a modern dance company going almost single-handed. And she's bought a number of my pieces, which speaks extremely well for her taste."

Eileen decided that she quite liked Samantha. Her frizzy blonde hair and black velvet thrift-shop thirties dress gave her a slightly silly air, but she was obviously very warm at heart and really quite clever. Vee would like her, Eileen thought—and that was certainly, to her own mind, the imprimatur of approval.

But Vee liked Matt. Called him the first most impossible man in the world—and clearly adored him.

Eileen shook her head. So much to think about. So much to sort out. So much to reconcile.

A snore came from the front seat: Alan had fallen asleep. Samantha giggled again. "I hope he knows who I am when he wakes up. Oh, look, Eileen. I do believe I behold the lights of civilization."

Alan sat bolt upright. "Ouch! My pouch! Not a couch!" he cried.

"Good heavens. He's gone bonkers," Samantha said.

"I'll explain later," Alan promised. He put an arm around Samantha's shoulders as she pulled the car to a halt in front of the Hotel Richemond. "Will you have a drink with me?"

"Oh, why not," Samantha answered. She handed the car keys to the doorman who helped her out. "Can we all have a drink together?"

"I'm going to bed," Eileen declared, as they walked into the main lobby.

"Come have just one with us in the bar. You can drink Coke if you've had enough booze," Alan pressed.

"Thanks, really, but I've got to go up and figure out some really delicate way to return *Monsieur* Longemalle's watch to him. And other such stuff. But I hope I'll see you again," she added to Samantha.

"Let's all have breakfast together," Samantha suggested blithely. She had a casual, unembarrassed air that Eileen envied. How much easier life would be if she could treat sex as just another facet of life, not a matter of thundering significance. Then, for a flashing instant of ecstasy, she remembered the way that stars had exploded when Matt had kissed her. Surely casual sex did not afford such glorious moments.

In any event, she told herself as the elevator lofted her upward, she was who she was. And being casual about sex was simply not part of the Eileen package.

She got to her room. She was exhausted, but she knew sleep would not be easy to come by. She changed into a nightgown and robe. Were she in her own apartment, she would have undertaken some mindless, soporific task like rearranging her bookselves or cleaning out her closet. Hotel life offered few such tasks. She plucked a wilted daisy from the arrangement of flowers that Jean-Claude Longemalle had sent her. She made a pass at neatening her already-neat toiletries. She looked out the window and noted that the snow seemed to be subsiding. She opened the book she'd been planning to read on the plane, but—despite her determined attempt to lose herself in someone else's story—she found that her attention was too fragmented for her to follow the plot.

Yet thinking about the problems most on her mind didn't

really work, either. She just didn't know how to bend her thoughts around the cataclysm called Matt Edwards. She could not imagine a life devoid of his presence. Yet she could not imagine that presence as anything but a thorn gouging deeply at her sensibilities.

She set her mind to a slightly less onerous task: trying to figure out how to return her beautiful Mont Blanc slip of a watch to Jean-Claude Longemalle without wounding him and jeopardizing his commitment to the Marsden Agency. She started several little speeches inside her head, but they just didn't work. This wasn't her night for clarity.

A knock sounded at her door. She caught her breath. She looked at her watch; it read two-fifteen. Who on earth could be calling? She went to the door and softly asked who was there.

"Alan. And Samantha. May we come in?"

She opened the door. Samantha was wearing a big plaid bathrobe of Alan's and a look of resoluteness on her round face. She gave Alan a little push on the back and said, "Don't just stand there, my good man. Let's go in."

"What's up?" Eileen asked, closing the door behind them. "Is something wrong?"

"We didn't wake you, did we?" Alan asked with unusual timidity.

"Never mind the amenities," Samantha snapped. She turned to Eileen. "Alan has something he wants to get off his chest. Don't you, Alan?"

"Um, Eileen, pal—" he started. He looked at Samantha as if begging for a reprieve.

"What is it, Alan?" Eileen asked.

"You remember this afternoon? When I called the office? In New York? And you came in and kept asking me what was wrong?"

"Yes, of course. *Was* something wrong? Are you okay?"

"Oh, I'm okay—" He sat down on her bed. He put his head in his hands. "I'm a crumb," he said. "I did something really low. Can you ever forgive me?"

Eileen sat next to him. She put a hand on his shoulder. "For heaven's sake, what happened? It can't be all that terrible."

"It's all that terrible," Samantha said grimly, folding her arms across her chest.

Alan looked at Eileen. He looked away. "I told them that the slogan for Mont Blanc was my idea," he got out. "I told them that "Buy time' was Alan Scott's genius idea."

"Oh." Eileen's voice was very small. She swallowed hard. Then she put her arms around Alan. "Never mind," she told him. "It's not the end of the world."

Samantha was still glaring. Alan looked at her and said to Eileen, "I told Samantha I'd call Marsden in the morning and tell him the truth."

Eileen thought for a moment. Then: "Don't do that. It would be an awfully hard thing to do. Really, it's not so important."

"It could make all the difference in your career, though. You could have gotten a lot of mileage out of it. A job on the creative end."

"Well," Eileen declared brightly, "if I had one good idea, I guess I'll have another, and I can ride that one to the top. If I don't have another good idea—I guess I don't belong in a better job."

"Eileen, do you mean it? Baby, you are one in a million." Alan shook his head in disbelief. "But it makes it even harder in a way. Can't you yell at me a little?"

"You rotten, no-good, low-down—" Eileen began, then she broke into laughter. "I can't really get mad enough. I guess I'm hurt that you betrayed our friendship, but I think I'm just finding out that I don't take advertising all that seriously. Maybe in a way you did me a service, Alan." She looked at him, at the boyish face, at the nervous way he was running his fingers through his hair. "But I have to know: Why did you do it? Why did you want that credit so badly? After you landed that big account in London and everything?"

"I don't know, really." He had the look now of a kid

who'd just been caught pouring fudge sauce over his mother's roses. "It just sort of happened. By chance you weren't here when I talked to Marsden, and—" He shrugged. "I guess subconsciously I was worried that with the economy the way it is Marsden might be tightening his belt, and I wanted to make sure that he thought I was just too valuable to let go."

"I still think," Samantha chimed in, "that he ought to make a clean breast of it."

Eileen shook her head. "I think the important thing is that he told you and that he told me."

"Told you because I made him," Samantha declared.

"You don't have to be Sigmund Freud to figure out that he probably told you because he was sure you would make him confess to me. Anyway, you know, he was right there talking with me when the idea was born. I don't know if you can say he was the father, but he was certainly the midwife. And when we get back to New York, he can lay it on thick with Marsden about how generally brilliant and charming and useful I was."

"You bet," Alan breathed, fervently. His color was the best Eileen had seen it all day. "The only trouble with that is," he added jovially, "they'll all assume we were sleeping together."

Eileen ruffled his hair. "That's the crass old Alan we all know and love. Now I'm sure you're okay." She said to Samantha, "Please take him away before he makes any more vulgar jokes. I'm a bit of a prude, you know."

"You're not!" Alan pounced. "You're a fantastic human being with a lot more spirit of give and take than the people I know who love dirty jokes and go to orgies and all the rest of that game."

"Careful," Samantha warned, "or you'll sleep alone tonight." But she was smiling.

Eileen hugged Alan, then impulsively put her arms around Samantha. She felt strangely uplifted. And finally ready to sleep.

chapter 17

EILEEN SLEPT UNTIL NOON, then woke to brilliant skies. Every trace of snow had vanished. The storm of the night before might never have been.

She wondered how Alan was feeling this morning. She decided it probably boded well for his state of mind—and his status with Samantha—that he hadn't yet telephoned. Some character, that Samantha: character in every sense of the word. Eileen found herself hoping that the young English potter wouldn't turn out to be just one more blonde in Alan's life. She gave every indication of being just the person he needed to inspire his graduation from playboyhood into real grown-up manhood. For all her breeziness about sex, she was still obviously a woman with a clear sense of right and wrong, with some direction to her thinking.

And speaking of being grown-up, Eileen said to herself, what about the phone call from Vee you didn't return?

No matter how complicated her feelings about Matt were, her affection for Vee was strong and simple. It was very well for her to decide that Vee would understand her silence, but that didn't really excuse her rudeness. And now that she'd had a solid night's sleep, she felt a little more on top of things, a little more capable of fielding the questions that the outspoken Vee might hurl at her.

Besides, Vee was surely the person in all the world who best understood Matt Edwards. She might close her eyes to some of his shortcomings, but very likely she would be perfectly eager to help Eileen understand the man whom

Alan, not unfairly, had dubbed The Stormy One. Eileen reminded herself that Vee had suggested a match between her and Matt before their accidental meeting. And Vee was not a stupid woman, not by any means. Eileen had poured her heart out to Vee on that flight to Geneva, had told Vee how bruising her ex-husband's conduct had been, how still violent she was on the subject of unfaithfulness. Yet Vee had envisioned Eileen and Matt together.

Unlikely though it seemed at this point, maybe Vee could help to build a bridge to span the huge gulf separating Eileen's and Matt's sexual values. Anything was better, Eileen thought, than spending the rest of her life looking across the chasm, yearning for what she wanted yet couldn't let herself have.

She put a call through to Vevey. Pierre answered. He greeted her warmly. He said that the kangaroo had arrived that morning and that Marie hadn't let go of it, she loved it so.

"Is Vee there?" Eileen asked.

"She already left for the airport. The Hong Kong flight leaves at two-fifteen. I know she was terribly eager to speak with you. Did you get her message?"

"I did. I just couldn't call her, Pierre."

"I understand," Pierre replied, and Eileen had the feeling he really did. "And so does Vee, I'm sure."

"When do you expect her back home?"

"She's due in Sunday morning around eight o'clock."

"That's some grueling schedule," Eileen commented.

"It is; but then she won't have to fly for a week, and she's looking forward to the chunk of time with Marie. And Helga's in her crew, so at least she has good company. Did you meet Helga?"

"Not exactly," Eileen murmured, glad that her blush wasn't transmittable by phone.

"She's a great friend of the family's."

"Yes, I know." Eileen visualized a blue chiffon scarf and felt her good mood eroding. "Well, I'm off to the museum."

"Be sure and see the Titians."

"Will you ask Vee to call me as soon as she's recovered from her trip? And give Marie an extra-big kiss for me."

Eileen took a long shower. She went to her closet and inspected her crimson velvet jeans, cleaned by the hotel valet after Marie's little mishap. They looked good as new. She put them on, along with the white silk shirt with cerise piping, also freshly cleaned. As she was placing her wallet, cosmetics, and other things she would need into the large shoulder bag she carried by day, her eye fell on the exquisite watch that had been bestowed on her the night before. She'd conveniently managed to put it out of her mind for a few hours. But now that she saw it, she realized the first order of business was returning it, with utmost tact, to Jean-Claude Longemalle. The Titians would have to wait a little while.

She called the Mont Blanc watch company offices and asked to be put through to the president's secretary. To her great surprise, *Monsieur* Longemalle answered his extension himself.

"But *monsieur*," she stammered, "I was certain that at this hour you would be out to lunch. I was calling your secretary to make an appointment with you."

"It is the other way around," he chuckled. "My secretary is out to lunch. You mentioned last night that I concern myself with every detail of running this business? How right you were. Unless I have a special engagement, I have a yogurt at my desk and take advantage of the midday lull."

"I'm sorry to have disturbed you," Eileen said.

"Not at all. Not at all. Charmed to hear your voice, my very dear *Mademoiselle* Connor. You wish to see me?"

"I do."

"It is always very agreeable to hear a beautiful young woman say with such intensity that she must see you. What time would suit you?"

"Whenever suits you, *monsieur*. If it could just be today, I'd be most grateful."

"Come right now, if that is convenient."

"You're sure I—"

"I'll expect you in twenty minutes, *mademoiselle*. You will, I take it, not be bringing Monsieur Scott?"

"No, it's—it's personal."

"Yes, I thought so," he said, in a voice she couldn't quite fathom.

Exactly twenty minutes later, Jean-Claude Longemalle was rising to greet her. "You are very charming in trousers," he commented gravely, kissing her hand. He ushered her into a massive mahogany chair thickly upholstered in pale gold velvet. He leaned against his desk. A shaft of light coming in through the window showed off the gleam of his silvery hair. It also rather cruelly played up the deep lines in his face, the pouches under his eyes. Still, Eileen thought, he was an impressive figure of a man. And for all the smoothness, even cockiness, that emanated from him, he looked—at least at this moment—endearingly vulnerable.

The speech she had rehearsed on her way over flew from her head. "I don't know how to begin," she said.

"Then let me begin for you." Jean-Claude Longemalle folded his arms across his chest. "You have come to return the watch, but you don't know how to do it without hurting my feelings and perhaps making me angry."

"You know that?" Eileen asked, astonished. "But how—"

"Please, *Mademoiselle* Connor, promise me something?"

"Yes, *monsieur*?"

"Do not ever play poker. You have a face that reveals all. I knew last night that you would not keep the watch. You only accepted it because—because of the nuances of the moment." He cleared his throat. "Do not think I am stupid. Or ungrateful."

"You are very kind, *Monsieur* Longemalle." Eileen unclapsed the watch, let her palm enjoy the delicate heft of the object one more time, then gave it to the watch company president. He set it down on his desk with all the ceremony befitting a discarded paper clip. "Look," Eileen burst out. "I also accepted it because it was a good business maneuver.

And almost didn't return it because I was afraid you might withdraw your account from the Marsden Agency."

Longemalle laughed. "You tell me nothing I didn't know. But the important thing is that you returned it anyway, even though you knew there was a risk. You just couldn't violate your own code ultimately. Would *Monsieur* Scott have done the same? If I had given him a watch that was anything but a trinket?"

Eileen thought about the way that Alan had betrayed her. But he'd confessed, hadn't he? Even without the jabbing finger of Samantha to spur him on, he would have had to confess before they returned to New York, wouldn't he have? "It might have taken him a little longer," she insisted loyally, "but in the end he would have done the same thing."

"I wonder." Then Longemalle laughed again. "We'll never know, will we?"

"I did tell him I was going to return the watch, and he didn't really argue."

"Didn't he? Well, good. Perhaps I misjudged the young man. Not that I thought him venal—only very weak. Not," he added, his eyes narrowing, "like the young man you fancy. The architect."

Eileen shivered. She felt as if she were in the presence of a wizard, a warlock. Or did her face simply give away everything?

"That is a man worthy of you," Longemalle declared.

"But—" Eileen shook her head. She couldn't finish. You didn't, after all, say to even the most self-assured of men: *But how can you talk so admiringly about the man who is sleeping with your wife?* Was Longemalle the ultimately generous soul? Or did he simply not care? She didn't know if she venerated him or despised him. As Alan had said, there was something disagreeable about men who collaborated in their wives' unfaithfulness.

After a few pleasantries and many declarations of mutual good will, Eileen and Longemalle shook hands—this time he chose, to her relief, to forego the kiss; and she left his sumptuously appointed office. As she got into the elevator, she noticed that the large square Mont Blanc clock in the corridor read exactly two-fifteen. Vee was just now taking off on the first leg of the Swissair flight to Hong Kong, if the plane was departing on time—and most likely it was departing precisely on time.

Eileen passed a series of cafés on her way toward the Museum of Art and History, on the Left Bank near the Old Town, and her stomach emphatically reminded her that she had had neither breakfast nor lunch. She ducked into a bustling little place called Le Quik Snak. In a sudden flurry of nostalgia, she ordered what the menu called "*le hamburg à l'Americaine.*" To her surprise, and then amusement, she was served an open-face hamburger with a sunny-side-up egg on top!

So many things in life, she mused, turned out not to be as advertised. So many things, and so many people. She thought of Alan with his swaggering playboy mannerisms on the surface and his scared little soul underneath. Then there was Samantha, almost his mirror opposite, with a dithery exterior and solid stuff underneath. Of all the people she'd been involved with in these tumultuous few days since she'd taken off from Kennedy Airport, really only Vee and Pierre and Marie had turned out to be exactly what they seemed to be. And even Vee had been something of a surprise. At first, Eileen reminded herself, she hadn't been able to see past Vee's flight attendant's uniform to the person underneath.

So many, many surprises this week. Incredible to think that she'd left New York on a Sunday night and here it was only Friday. In a way she'd had a lifetime's worth of experiences. And her trip wasn't over yet. Who knew what shocks—pleasant or unpleasant—still lurked? One thing was certain. She'd been absolutely right in her almost mystical certainty that her life was going to take a right-angle turn in Geneva.

For the better. No matter what happened with the tall stranger that the world had sent her way. Change was always ultimately for the better, wasn't it?

Another thing was certain: She had grown. She had stopped demanding that people be simple, that she herself be simple. In a way the turning point had been the brief train trip with Alan when she'd been able to admit to herself, and to him, that she wanted him to want her even though she didn't want him. She'd even been able to joke about it. Just a few days earlier that would have been impossible.

Geneva had opened her up in some way. The strange, seductive angles of the streets of the Old Town had forced her to view life from a different perspective.

Yet some fundamentals remained concrete-firm, and that was good, too. She had principles, she had standards, she had certain psychological needs, and she had the sense to honor them and not pretend they weren't there, even when they vastly complicated matters. To deny them would merely be to postpone trouble.

Would she forever be caught in a conflict between her basic commitments, her basic needs, and her gargantuan longing for Matt? She drank deeply of mineral water, as though to wash away the dread possibility. It stayed firmly anchored in mind, the knot she'd been trying to unravel for days ever since she'd understood the terrible difference between them. He wanted to tack her onto his life. She wanted him to replace all others in her life. There it was, large and immutable as the mountains.

On the other hand—so many other hands that she might have been an octopus!—they so clearly shared a cornucopia of beliefs. Even that very first morning, eating breakfast at the Clemence and arguing about everything under the sun, she'd felt a fierce kinship with him. They were of the same breed, on the same team.

Except for that one damnable difference.

She ate the last bit of her *hamburg à l'Americaine*—strange but delicious and satisfying, paid her bill, then headed to the museum. She sought out the Titians as Pierre had counseled, and then lingered in front of the Corot and Pissarro landscapes for which the museum was also renowned. The lyrical single-mindedness of the Corots and the mellow light of the Pissarros refreshed and strengthened her. She paused for a moment to reflect on her own work in the world. Would she ever give anyone even a tiny fraction of the pleasure these paintings gave to her?

She looked at the paintings, admired them, and wished with all her heart that Matt was there to expostulate about them and argue with her about them. About them and everything else. Oh, the joy of arguing with an ally!

When she got out of the museum dusk was descending. She'd spent longer looking at paintings than she'd realized. She glanced down at her wrist, instantly realized how silly the gesture was, and laughed at herself. Then she thought, Maybe the moment had come for her to buy time for herself. She hadn't spent all her special fund on clothes. She might not be able to afford a Mont Blanc quartz crystal watch, but surely she could find one within her means. She heard the cathedral bells announce five o'clock. If she hurried, she could make her purchase before the shops closed up for the day. She decided to try her luck at the big department store where she'd found the stuffed kangaroo for Marie. They'd probably have a bigger selection than the specialty shops, especially in her price range.

As Eileen entered the huge store, she noticed an intense group of people clustered around the counter where miniaturized TV sets were on special sale. Something about the configuration of the crowd frightened her. It reminded her of the old newsreel clips of people glued to big radio sets during World War Two, waiting for the latest bulletin.

Heart speeding up, she went to join the crowd and see what they were seeing on the tiny TV screens. She hoped that there hadn't been a major flare-up in the Middle East. Her concern was for the stability of the world; but it also had a more personal side. Her father was still young enough to be called back to active duty if the United States got into a military conflict.

By the time she got to the counter, the crowd was dispersing. The newscaster whose face they'd been watching on multiple screens was droning on about the economy.

"What happened?" she asked a saleswoman. "What was the news that everyone was watching a minute ago?"

The saleswoman shook her head. "It's a disgrace, isn't it? That they can't control these things?"

"Please." Eileen's heart was pounding so hard, she could hear it. "Tell me. Please."

"I thought they had all those devices," the saleswoman said. "Lord knows, the average honest citizen can't go anywhere without all kinds of hassle."

Eileen wanted to shake the earnest gray-haired woman. She leaned across the counter. "Will you please tell me what happened?" she asked. "Please?"

"Didn't you hear? There was a hijacking."

Eileen closed her eyes in a futile attempt to stem the tide of nausea that suddenly washed over her. "What airline? What flight? Do you kno

"One of ours," the saleswoman said. Eileen suppressed a moan. "The Swissair two-fifteen flight to Hong Kong."

chapter 18

EILEEN FAIRLY FLEW to the nearest coin phone. With trembling hands she searched through her bag for her address book. She turned to the L's, then realized that she hadn't yet transferred Vee's telephone number from the message slip given her by the desk clerk. It was still on the bedside table back in her hotel room. Cursing herself, she dialed information, said she needed a number in Vevey, wrote it down in her book when the operator delivered it, hung up, checked the printed instructions for calling long distance, and finally, feeling as though whole hours had passed, dialed the correct sequence of numbers.

Busy.

She leaned against the wall of the phone booth, drew ten deep breaths, dialed again.

Still busy.

She felt at an absolute loss. She didn't know where to turn. After dismissing a couple of absurd thoughts—like calling her mother—she decided to call Alan. She got the Hotel Richemond on the phone and asked for *Monsieur* Scott.

No answer.

She was grinding her teeth now. The phone booth felt suffocatingly hot. She tried Vevey again, got a busy signal again, and decided to leave. She ran out of the store so fast that she half expected to be accosted as a shoplifter. She ran across the Mont Blanc Bridge. She ran up the Quai du Mont Blanc to the hotel, ran across the lobby, leaped into an elevator just as the doors were closing, ran down the corridor, let herself into her room, and collapsed on her bed. She allowed herself one minute of respite, then stood up and started throwing essentials into the smaller of her two suitcases.

She tried Vee's number. Busy.

She snatched up a train schedule she'd put in her purse Wednesday night. There was a seven-ten train to Vevey. If she hurried, she would just make it. She sat down to write a brief note to Alan.

The telephone jangled. She snatched the receiver off the hook.

It was Pierre.

"Pierre!" she cried. "Are you okay? What can I do? I've been trying you frantically."

"We've been trying you. Didn't you get our messages?"

"I was in such a hurry to get to my room when I got back to the hotel, I forgot to check. Look, may I come up there?"

"Would you please?" Relief lightened the terrible tension in his voice. "Marie can tell something isn't right, though we're doing our best to behave normally. She loves you. It would be wonderful if you came."

"I'll get the seven-ten train. Don't bother to meet me. I remember the way up. Do you need anything?"

"No, our housekeeper, Coco, is here, and she's so distraught I keep making up errands for her and sending her into town to keep her from moping around the house."

"Is there— Is there any more news?"

"We don't know a thing," Pierre said. "By the time you get here, maybe we will. It'll be all right, Eileen. You know, we all live with the notion in the backs of our minds that someday this will happen. I know how calm Vee is in a crisis, and Helga is very good too."

"If I know Vee," Eileen declared, "she's already got the hijacker sitting down, having coffee, and discussing his love life. She'll probably try to fix him up with me, in fact!"

She got a real chuckle out of Pierre, then hung up and finished her note to Alan. Despite the brave words she and Pierre had exchanged, tears kept springing to her eyes. One fell on her note and made a blue, inky puddle of the "D" in "Dear Alan."

She gathered her belongings, took the elevator down to the lobby, left the message for Alan, accepted her own messages from the desk clerk, then went to the doorman and asked for a cab. The train station was really within walking distance, but she felt a sudden deep exhaustion that made the idea of even a short walk about as appealing as the thought of a climb up Mont Blanc.

She bought a copy of an evening paper, scanned page one, found nothing. Apparently it had gone to press before news of the hijacking had gotten out. She asked a teenager with a transistor radio if he had heard any late bulletins; he shook his head at her French and said, *"Deutsch."* She asked him again in German, and he said he hadn't heard anything all day but music. She gave up in disgust and walked away.

The ticket seller asked her if she wanted Vevey round-trip or one-way. The question upset her so much that she couldn't answer right away, and—misunderstanding her silence—the ticket seller repeated his question in English. She finally asked for a one-way ticket because of course she had no way of knowing when she'd be coming back.

Vee. Be okay. Please be okay.

The Lakeside train trip seemed interminable. She tried to read the newspaper she'd bought, but concentration was hard to come by. She looked at the faces of the other passengers and tried to imagine their names, their stories, what towns they would get off in; that game quickly palled.

Vee. What are you feeling? Is your mouth dry with fear, the way mine is? Please, please be okay.

Despite her instructions, Pierre met her train. Marie was in a frame-pack on his back, fast asleep.

"She insisted we meet you," the tall, balding, eternally

warm man explained, hugging Eileen. "Then the minute we got out into the cold air, she felt asleep. You're lovely to come."

"You're lovely to let me come," Eileen declared, as they walked toward the Lenkes' house. "I'd have worn out the carpet in my hotel room pacing if you hadn't."

"We've had some news," Pierre said.

"Yes?" Eileen eagerly clutched his arm.

"Apparently there's only one hijacker involved."

"That's good, isn't it?"

"Well, it's good in the sense that it means there isn't some very well-orchestrated political event going on," Pierre said cautiously. "But one guy alone means— Well, you have to worry a little bit that it's a real nut. In any event," he went on hastily, "he wants the plane to fly to Bogota."

"Bogota?" Again Eileen tried desperately to interpret that in their favor. "Thank God it's not the Middle East or Cuba or some other hot spot."

"Amen," Pierre said.

"They'll have to— Won't they have to refuel?" Eileen asked. She couldn't make up her mind if that was a good or bad thing.

"Yes. The Hong Kong flight was supposed to refuel in Bombay, so they'll have to touch down," looking at his watch, "in a couple of hours or so. They'll probably aim for Dakar. That's the usual stopping-off place on South American flights."

"What equipment are they flying?" It seemed important to Eileen to know every possible detail, as though knowledge would give her a modicum of control over the wild situation.

"A DC-10. It's Vee's and Helga's favorite aircraft," he added, a slight tremor in his voice.

At that moment the sleeping bundle on his back stirred, stretched, and cried out, happily, "Eileen!"

"Hello, darling Marie." Eileen bestowed a fat kiss on Marie's elfin nose.

"Eileen, Eileen, Eileen!" Marie repeated, stressing the first syllable in a way that made Eileen's heart turn over.

Her emotions were already so close to breakpoint that when Matt Edwards opened the door of the Lenkes' house and greeted them, she scarcely reacted. He took the baby-carrier off his brother-in-law's back and extricated Marie as Pierre helped Eileen off with her coat.

"Any news?" Pierre asked.

Matt shook his dark head. "But I hope you worked up an appetite on your walk. I got Coco cooking as therapy, and she's produced enough for a small army."

Eileen smiled weakly. The thought of food was ghastly.

Pierre started upstairs with Eileen's suitcase. "Matt has the big guest room," he said, "but there's another small room next to ours where you'll be comfortable, I'm sure."

"I'll move out to my studio," Matt thundered, as though the question of where Eileen slept were somehow an assault.

"Why don't you put me in with Marie?" Eileen suggested. "There's a cot in her room, isn't there?"

"The first instance in history," Matt muttered, "of a grown woman having a two-year-old for a chaperone."

Eileen turned to him with her sweetest smile and asked, "Is there only one topic ever on your mind?"

"Apparently it's plenty on your mind."

"As it happens, I'd like to room with Marie so I'll be there in case she wakes up during the night."

"She doesn't wake up at night," Matt said. "She's famous for it. Getting her to sleep isn't always easy, but once you get her there, she stays there."

"Under ordinary circumstances," Eileen retorted. "But how do you know what vibrations she's picking up? Then, too, Vee told me she's teething and . . ."

"I think Eileen has a good idea," Pierre interrupted. "Anyway, it'll be a treat for Marie to wake up in the morning and find Eileen there even if she doesn't get up during the night. Matt, why don't you take Eileen into the kitchen and introduce her to Coco," he added, in a none-too-subtle attempt at defusing the atmosphere.

Matt's silence, as he led Eileen through the dining room, was so out of keeping with what she knew of him that it seemed in a way as thundering as the angriest of his voices.

"I suppose," she said, "that it would be nice for Pierre if we managed not to grapple at each other's throats all the time. He's got enough on his mind."

"He's not the only one," Matt snapped.

"Yes, of course. I'm sorry. I know how attached you are to your sister. And to Helga."

He gave her a withering glance but didn't say anything. He pushed opened the swinging door to the kitchen. The big white room with its stainless steel counters was dazzling after the dark elegance of the dining room. Eileen wondered, as she had the first time she visited the house, if that sharp contrast had been deliberately designed by Matt. In a way, it seemed to mirror the contrasts within his own personality.

"Coco, this is Eileen," Matt said, and Eileen found both her hands being grasped by a short, very round woman whose contours reminded Eileen of a cookie jar one of her grandmothers had owned. Coco's smooth, sweet face could almost have been a cookie itself. Eileen guessed her age at sixty-five or so, and couldn't help mentally contrasting her with Jean-Claude Longemalle, perhaps some ten years her senior. Longemalle, with the help of expert tailors, barbers, valets, and probably a very disciplined routine of exercises, concealed his age—or at least contained it. Coco flaunted her years, just as she simply let her weight hang out. Here was a woman clearly incapable of guile on any level. Eileen immediately adored her and felt comforted by her presence, her existence.

"Our poor Vee," Coco exclaimed, in the singsong French of the native Genevoise.

"It's a terrible business," Eileen said, "but can you think of anyone capable of handling it better than Vee? Probably the number-one worry on her mind is what's going on with all of us back here."

Coco dabbed at her eyes with the corner of her apron. "I know, but—"

"Eileen is right," Matt interjected crisply. "Can you imagine Vee's horror at the thought that a guest had been in her home for fifteen minutes and no one had offered her a drink? Just because of some stupid hijacker who's probably already wishing he'd taken the train instead of flying? Eileen, what can I get you?"

"If there's more of Pierre's white wine—"

"Merely a cellar full." He let his hand rest lightly on her back for one exquisite second, then set off for the wine bins.

"I can't believe how many different good smells there are in here." Despite the terrible knot of anxiety in her stomach, and the feeling that it was somehow indecent to eat when Vee was in such dire straits, Eileen was actually beginning to get some appetite. "Does my nose fool me, or do I smell an apple tart?"

"You do indeed!" Coco beamed. She opened an oven and pulled out a rack to allow Eileen a glimpse of a classic, flat, square open-faced tart, the slices of apples arranged in pristine rows and browning delicately under an apricot glaze.

"That's heavenly looking. I'm not a bad cook, but pastry has always been my weak spot. I just lack that light touch with a rolling pin. What else is cooking in here? Wait, Coco, let me guess." She wrinkled her nose. "Some kind of stew. Beef—no, more delicate than that. Veal."

"This young lady is a genius!" Coco exclaimed to Matt, as he returned bearing a long-stemmed goblet for Eillen. "At least her nose is. She's a regular detective, she is. Unless you told her, Matt." She put her hands on her considerable hips and glared at Matt.

"Not me, Coco. Innocent," Matt insisted, in his hopelessly bad French. "You're right. She is a genius. I could have told you that."

Eileen took a sip of wine. "To think I thought that the Neuchâtel I had on the plane was the ultimate in pure wines. This tastes like something that sprang up out of the earth without any human interference. I don't understand why

Swiss wines aren't all the rage in New York. The French white wine I've had has been sort of crude, compared to this."

"I can just hear your Madison Avenue crowd 'proclaiming' their Chablis and their Pouilly-Fuissé," Matt glowered. Then he added, in gentler tones, "Swiss wines don't travel well. Too fragile. Oh, you can buy some fairly good Neuchâtel in the States, and once I had a halfway decent bottle of Fendant, which is closer to Pierre's wine, but to my mind it's better to just drink this stuff while you're here and then remember it while you're away from it." He gave Eileen a look of such intensity that Coco bustled off to the farthest corner of the kitchen. "I'm a good rememberer," he told her. "Are you?"

"Yes."

Their eyes met; their lips hastened to follow. Then there came a pounding on the kitchen door.

"Marie," muttered Matt. "She can't quite push the door open yet." He laid a finger against Eileen's cheek, then went to let his niece in.

The redheaded toddler threw her arms around Eileen's knees. "Pouch story!" she cried.

"Where's your new kangaroo? We'll tell it the story, too."

"Living room," Marie said.

Eileen scooped her up. "Then we'll go to the living room. See you later, Coco." As she carried Marie back out through the dining room and across the hallway, the little girl reminded her so much of Vee that she felt a pang near her heart. Here they all were, talking about wine and behaving almost as if things were normal, and there was Vee, trapped high up in the sky with a madman. But life was like that. One carried on.

"Where is Pierre?" Eileen asked Matt.

"Upstairs talking to some friends in Interpol to see if he can get any inside information. That's pretty good, the way you can carry a baby and a wine glass without dropping either. Had a lot of practice?"

"Not on either account. I'm an only child, so there aren't any nieces or nephews. When I was growing up we never lived anyplace long enough for me to get to know any babies. And my neighborhood in New York seems to be composed exclusively of single men and women in their twenties and thirties."

"I suppose you're too wrapped up in your career," Matt said, unable to keep the scorn from his voice, "to think about having your own children. Especially now, after your big coup. You'll be promoted, I expect."

"Oh, I—" Eileen began. Then body and voice came to a halt as they reached the living room. She drew a deep breath. "Matt. That painting over the fireplace. It's new, isn't it." She stared at the huge canvas full of exploding circles and ovals in a vast range of reds. The shapes seemed to have been hurled, not stroked, onto the canvas. The painting could have been called "The Creation of the World." Or, no less aptly, "The End of the World."

"New painting!" Marie cried out. She wriggled out of Eileen's arms and ran across the room, pointing.

Matt leaned against the doorway. "Like it?" he inquired, in his most casual drawl.

"Like it? *Like* doesn't seem the right word at all. I liked the Pissarros and Corots I saw at the museum this afternoon. This painting demands a much stronger response. I love it. I hate it." She shivered. "I feel owned by it. Those circles are the planet, but they're also me." She felt the color rising in her cheeks. She added hastily, "I don't mean that I think you painted it about me. It's just that it's so powerful, so intimate somehow." She suddenly had the feeling that she'd given much too much away. She called out to Marie, "Do you like the new painting, honey?"

"Pretty!" Marie exclaimed, and Matt and Eileen laughed tenderly.

"I started it Monday night," Matt said, his voice still completely offhand. Then, before Eileen could respond, he started bounding up the stairs. "I think I'll go see how Pierre is doing."

Marie scampered over to Eileen and threw chubby little arms around her knees. "Story. Tell story."

"Of course, darling. Where's your kanagroo? Oh, there it is." Eileen gathered up child and toy and snuggled down into a leather armchair. She told the tale of Blippy's pouch three times. By the third time, Marie's breathing had deepened, her thumb was in her mouth, and her head lay heavily against Eileen's chest. The moment was so sweet and full that Eileen could scarcely bear to move. But clearly her little friend was ready for bed.

Holding her close, trying not to jar her, Eileen carried Marie up to the nursey.

Marie opened her eyes. "Mama?" she said.

"Shhh, darling. Eileen is here. I'm just going to change your diaper and slip on your pajamas."

"Pajamas," Marie repeated sleepily.

Eileen quickly had Marie all set for the night. She tucked the baby into the crib. She bestowed kisses. She hovered for a moment, turned on the night light, saw that Marie was fast asleep, and went downstairs.

Coco came into the living room to say that dinner was ready. Pierre and Matt appeared a moment later with some rather more startling news.

Vee's plane had landed in Dakar.

chapter 19

COCO HAD PUT candles on the dining-room table. Vee would have wanted it that way, she insisted.

Eileen suppressed a shudder. To her mind the candles were macabre, not festive.

Coco ladled out veal stew and put a mound of the tiny Swiss dumplings, the famous *spätzle*, on each plate. Matt went around the table pouring white wine. And Pierre, in a voice that Eileen found unnervingly calm, conveyed the latest information on the hijacking.

The plane had landed at Dakar to take on fuel. Authorities were going to try to persuade the hijacker to release the passengers and some of the crew. They were also going to try to find out more about who the hijacker was and what he wanted, since his motives remained murky.

Coco suddenly put her apron up over her face and sobbed.

"Coco," Matt said sternly, "you have to pull yourself together. Think of Pierre. Don't make it harder, darling Coco."

"But our Vee, our sweet Vee," the housekeeper sobbed. Then she asked wildly, "The authorities won't try to do anything crazy, will they? Tell me they won't. There won't be any guns, will there? They won't try to shoot out the tires, will they, Pierre?"

"I'm not sure that isn't just what they ought to do," Matt said wearily. He pushed his plate away. "Delicious, Coco, but I just can't."

"Now, Matt, you have to keep up your strength. Just a little bit more, there's a good boy."

Obediently Matt ate another piece of veal. Eileen forced herself to pace him. Forks and knives clicked on china and echoed eerily in the big room.

So big without Vee to help fill it up. A terrible cave without Vee.

"Then it's on to Bogota?" Eileen asked, aiming for a conversational tone, as if she were discussing someone's long-awaited vacation.

"Yes. The Colombian authorities have already given permission for the landing. They'll have a special runway cleared. There will be time for— for the things they couldn't prepare for at Dakar."

Eileen nodded. She didn't press for details. She wasn't sure she wanted to hear them.

Coco cleared the table, brought in the apple tart, and served it. Eileen, Matt, and Pierre all mustered lavish compliments to the cook; then a terrible silence fell.

"Let's have coffee in the living room, shall we?" Matt finally said. "I need to pace."

"Good idea," Pierre said. "Delicious meal, Coco. Sorry we didn't do it more justice."

"Can you imagine the feast I'll prepare when our Vee comes home?" Coco cried. Then she hastened off to the kitchen, where, Eileen suspected, she was going to have another good cry.

Eileen ran upstairs to check on Marie. The baby was sleeping soundly. Eileen stroked the fine red hair, adjusted a coverlet, cast up a brief but fervent prayer for the safe return of Marie's mama, then went back downstairs.

"It's such a comfort to have you here, Eileen," Pierre said.

"Marie is such a wonderful child. Magical, really. You're all so wonderful."

"All of us?" Matt drawled, forcing flame to her cheeks again. Then he said, "Let's try the radio and TV, Pierre, and see if we can pick up any bulletins."

"My friend in Interpol promised to call me as soon

as—" Pierre's sentence hung unfinished in midair, interrupted by the heart-stopping jangling of a telephone.

Matt was nearest. He grabbed up the receiver. "Hello?" Then "Yes," he tersely barked twice and handed the phone to Eileen. "For you," he said, a disgusted look on his face.

The caller was Alan Scott. He'd just received Eileen's note. Was there anything at all he could do? he asked.

"I don't think so. I just wanted you to know where I'd gone."

"I saw something about the hijacking on TV, but they didn't mention the names of the crew, and I didn't put it all together. Gee, that's just rotten. Tell Pierre how sorry I am."

"I will. I'd better get off the phone now in case someone from the airline calls. I'll be here until—well, until." She hung up.

"I hope," Matt Edwards said, "that he doesn't have to do anything really challenging before you get back. Like cross the street or tie his shoelaces, for instance."

"Oh, Matt. Why do you dislike him so?"

"He's dangerous. Weak men are always the real killers."

"And you have no weaknesses?" Eileen challenged him. "You wouldn't call Régine Longemalle a weakness?"

"Régine Longemalle?" he echoed in astonishment. "She's hardly the woman on my mind right now."

No, Eileen thought bitterly, Helga Winter is the woman on your mind tonight. Then she felt a wave of self-disgust. How could she be jealous of a woman who was at that very moment undergoing a terrible trial?

Coco appeared just then, carrying a heavy silver tray laden with a large *café filtre* pot, small cups, a bowl of sugar cubes, strips of lemon rind, and a bottle of anisette liqueur. "How do you take it, Eileen?" she asked.

"What does the house recommend?"

"Matt and Pierre like a splash of anisette, and lemon rind rubbed around the rim of the cup. No sugar."

"That sounds good to me. Oh, thank you, Coco. Delicious."

The telephone rang again. Eileen's hand shook so that

her *demi-tasse* rattled in its saucer. Again Matt answered. This time he quickly handed the phone to Pierre. The others stared raptly as Pierre listened, made a few staccato comments, and hung up.

"Well, I have a little good news," he reported. He smiled weakly. "The gunman let the passengers deplane in Dakar. And they report that he was very courteous and seems relatively calm and stable. But—" The smiled faded. "The gunman would not release any of the crew. So Vee and Helga are now on their way to sunny Bogota."

Matt let loose a one-word expletive.

"We might as well go to sleep," Pierre said. "Or get drunk or play poker or whatever. There won't be any more news until the morning."

He put his face in his hands.

chapter 20

THE IDEA OF SLEEPING, like the idea of eating, was almost an obscenity in a crisis, Eileen concluded. It was as though Vee somehow could be helped if the people who loved her concentrated on her agonizing plight instead of escaping into unconsciousness. But—like eating—sleeping was very necessary at such times. One had to keep up one's strength.

Deciding that sleep was a good idea didn't mean that sleep was within her grasp. Eileen envisioned getting into bed and staring for hours at the shadows on the ceiling of the nursery. She decided to take a long bath in an effort to relax a little. Coco gave her thick towels and a container of Swiss bath oil that smelled faintly of pine and was supposed to make tense muscles relax. Eileen lingered in the fragrant suds for half an hour. By the time she'd dried herself off, put on a nightgown, and slid between the flowered sheets on the cot in Marie's room, Eileen actually did feel relaxed. Marie's even breathing was a kind of wind symphony that eased her one notch further. Despite the terrible weight on her mind, she quickly fell asleep.

Unconsciousness was no escape, however. Her dreams were horrible. Giant, menacing birds filled the skies of her mind. And Vee was screaming—

No. Marie was crying.

Eileen was at her crib in a flash. She gathered the baby up into her arms and rocked her, murmuring soothing words.

"Mama, mama," Marie cried.

"It's all right, darling. You know your mama often goes away. But she loves you very much, and she always comes

back, and she'll come back this time, too." She smoothed
the fine red hair back from the baby's damp forehead. She
sat down in a big old-fashioned rocking chair and worked
up a rhythmic motion.

Marie's sobs grew less intense. "Bottle," she hiccuped.

Eileen looked around the dark room. She had no idea
where the bottles were kept. She wondered if Marie could
drink from a cup. There was a cup in the bathroom. Or
maybe there were bottles in the kitchen, if she could find
her way down there without rousing the whole household.

"Is there anything a mere uncle can do?" a voice asked
from the doorway. A startled Eileen looked up to see Matt,
wearing a pair of jeans and nothing else. "Forgive my in-
decorous attire," he drawled, "but I thought it was more
important to go for milk than to bother with a shirt." He
handed a bottle to Marie. She grabbed it eagerly and lay
sucking at it contentedly in Eileen's arms.

"Thank you," Eileen said. "I had no idea where the
bottles were. You've saved the hour."

"The kindest words I've ever heard from your sweet
lips," Matt said. He stood in the doorway, arms folded
across his chest. "You two make a pretty scene. If I went
in for painting madonna-and-child scenes, I'd ask you to
pose."

Eileen looked down at Marie. "Such a sweet child. Funny
how much younger she seemed when she woke up, crying
for her mama and bottle."

"They regress when they're afraid. Don't we all?"

"I guess so," Eileen answered softly. "In fact, when I
heard about the hijacking, my immediate impulse was to
call my own mama."

Matt nodded. "You're lucky to have a mama. We lost
our parents in a plane crash when Vee was twenty-one and
I was sixteen."

"A plane crash!" Eileen hugged Marie close.

"Yes. Vee had just started at flight attendants' school.
She decided to go on with her training anyway. She said
it was either that or give in to fear and become a kind of

living ghost. I sweated plenty the first couple of times she flew, but I got over it, the way she said I would. I think, by the way, that the wee beastie in your arms is fast asleep."

Eileen settled Marie into her crib, then extricated the bottle the toddler still was clutching. "This should go into the refrigerator," she said to Matt. "I'll take it down, if you'll tell me where the lights are."

"I'll take it down. You get back to sleep. Unless—unless you feel like talking?"

The tentativeness in his voice was so unlike anything she'd ever heard from Matt that all of Eileen's defenses crumbled. She suddenly stopped seeing him in relation to herself and perceived him as a man whose closest kin was in mortal danger. And to make the horrific situation even worse, that danger held especially dark connotations for him.

"Actually, I'm so awake now, I don't think I could sleep if I tried," Eileen said, truthfully enough. She picked her robe up from the chair next to the cot and pulled it around her.

"Good." Matt's voice was almost brisk again. "I think a talk is long overdue. Let me just stop in the guest room and get a sweater. The trouble with these big old houses is that no matter how much insulation you pack in, they're always a little drafty."

"Did I say drafty?" Matt inquired a few moments later. "It's downright cold." He and Eileen were in the living room. The robe she was wearing was scant protection against the winter chill that had seeped into the house; and Matt, now wearing a forest green turtleneck sweater with his jeans, didn't seem much more comfortable. "I think I'll light a small fire," he said. He knelt at the hearth and busied himself with kindling. A cheery, warming blaze rushed into life almost instantly.

"When I was a teenager," Eileen commented, settling into the leather armchair where earlier she'd told the story of Blippy's pouch to Marie, "the ability to build a fire was one of my tests for men—or boys, I guess I should say."

Matt laughed. "Typical romantic teen thinking. Was it a good test?"

"Of course not. Those things never are. I met too many guys who could build a fire but didn't have the general competency I thought it signaled."

"Was your ex-husband a good fire-builder?"

Eileen caught her breath. "In fact he was, which perfectly demonstrates the weakness of the test."

"Maybe it just holds in the negative. There are men who can build fires who aren't great, but there are no great men who can't build fires. His voice was jabbing at her again, like a boxer's fist. Was there never to be more than a moment's peace between them? Eileen wondered. "I bet anything," Matt went on, "that Alan Scott is incapable of building a fire. He'd be too nervous about getting dirt under his fingernails. Besides, his mother probably told him that playing with matches is naughty."

"Oh, do please stop carrying on about Alan Scott!" Eileen cried. "Aren't there more worthy targets of your scorn?"

"He's going to hurt you. I'm certain of it. You think he's safe, safer than I am, but I warn you: He's the dangerous one."

Eileen thought about what Alan had done to her by claiming credit for the "Buy Time" slogan. It had been a low, disloyal act, no doubt about it. But had he really damaged her? No. Nor could he. She just wasn't vulnerable to him in any important way. "No," she insisted softly to Matt. "He's not going to hurt me."

"But I am?" Matt crossed swiftly to the chair where Eileen was sitting. "Do you know," he asked, grabbing Eileen's hand, "How much I want you?"

Eileen gently withdrew her hands. "Please, Matt."

"Please, Matt. Please, Matt," he mimicked. "Damn it, lady, I have felt your heart race when I kissed you. I've heard your blood sizzle when I touched you. Why do you deny your own feelings?"

"What makes you think I do?" Eileen murmured. The
fire Matt had built hissed and crackled. "But having feelings
is one thing. Giving in to them is another."

Matt stood straight, tall, and utterly still in front of her.
His face was a mask of impassivity. "Once and forever, let
me understand you. You think desire is the devil's ploy?
You think sex is somehow evil?"

"Evil?" Eileen made no effort to keep the astonishment
from her countenance and voice. "Evil? Oh, it can be used
for evil ends, like almost anything else. But I'm no puritan,
Matt. To my mind sex is a celebration of life, of the dance
of the cosmos. That's why I value it. That's why I take it
seriously. That's why I won't share it except—" Her voice
quavered. "Except with someone who values it as much as
I do. That's why I can't," looking down, "make love with
a promiscuous man. My whole nature rebels against it. Not
because I think sex is bad; because I think it's so good."

"And you think I—" He slowly shook his head. "Is the
word *trust* nowhere in your vocabulary?"

She shivered, and this time not from the cold. "That
word can be one of the most dreadful weapons in the English
language. That's what Keith kept saying to me. My ex-
husband. 'Trust me. I love you. I won't leave you.' But
that didn't mean he was willing to give up his—his friend
for me. Or maybe 'friends' is more apt. Perhaps if I'd
played the game his way, he wouldn't have left me. But
what would I have had? Part-time companionship, half-
hearted loyalty. I know there are women and men who can
live with that. I don't condemn them. They're not immoral
in my mind. But where's the celebration? Where's the sense
of specialness?"

There was a sound that Eileen could have sworn came
from grinding teeth. "If Keith came back now and told you
that he'd seen the error of his ways and he couldn't live
without you and he would henceforth foresake all others,
I suppose you'd take him back. Since apparently his promiscuity, as you put it, was all that stood between you."

"Oh, no, it wasn't just his promiscuity."

"Would you?" Matt asked impatiently. "Would you take him back?"

A lone motorcycle roared by, breaking the silence of the night. Eileen tracked the sound until she couldn't hear it anymore. "I used to have fantasies of that," she said, dreamily. "Keith returning all repentant."

"So it's what you want," Matt said, with a harshness that startled her.

"No. Not anymore. I guess for a while I did because I was lonely, and my ego was hurt. After all, if he loved me so much, why was he willing to give up so little for me?"

"Maybe he couldn't give up his nature any more than you could give up yours."

Eileen looked Matt straight in the eye. His pupils sparkled with reflected light from the dancing flames in the fireplace. "No, I suppose not," she said sadly. "But that's not the only thing. You see, my life with Keith was sort of—a sleepwalker's dream. Then a little while ago I woke up. And being awake was so exquisite that I knew I could never again be totally happy with Keith or anyone like him. Which may mean that I'm going to spend my life pretty much on my own. Either that, or slowly forget what being awake felt like and make one of those awful compromises with life. Because the one totally awake man I know, the man who made me wake up, happens to want a number of other women as much as he wants me. And I don't think—" She couldn't finish the sentence. She said instead, "I've talked an awful lot, Matt, haven't I? My throat is dry as anything."

"I'll get you some cognac."

"Actually, would there be a Coke in the house? That would feel best of all."

"As it happens, not even eight happy years of marriage to a vintner has cured my sister of the belief that Coke is one of the ten great inventions since the beginning of time. I'll get you one."

Alone in front of the roaring fire, Eileen drew a deep

breath. In a way it felt good to have poured her heart out to Matt. Yet there was something miserable-making about having so clearly delineated the great gulf between them. For a wild moment she almost wished he would lie to her, fool her for one night, so that she could know the ultimate bliss of giving herself to him. But of course he wouldn't do that. He was a womanizer; he was also a man of honor.

He brought her a Coke on ice with a slice of lemon, the way she most liked it, in a great goblet worthy of a vintage wine. She gulped at it gratefully. He went over to the bar in the corner of the living room and poured out a tot of cognac for himself. Then he stood with his back to her, meditatively staring at the fire.

His silence was so unusual as to classify, in Eileen's mind, as an event. Perhaps he was thinking about Vee and Helga. Eileen wondered what time it was, and exactly where over land or sea the two women were. She also couldn't help wondering what effect the hijacking would have on Matt's relationship with Helga. It might well be a kind of catalyst. It might even precipitate a marriage. Helga would probably be a perfect wife for Matt, Eileen decided in some dispassionate corner of her mind. A traveler, like him; someone who would give him plenty of space to do his own thing. And it certainly weighed heavily in her favor that she was such a good friend of Vee's.

Vee. Helga. Please be okay, she prayed silently. Then she said out loud, "Matt?"

"Yes?"

"Do you feel like talking? I'm a pretty good listener."

"All set to be my boon confidante, eh?" he asked sarcastically.

"I didn't mean to intrude on your thoughts. But if you need to let off steam—"

"Let off steam!" He whirled around. He bent over her. His fingers sought their old niches in her shoulders. "I'll tell you how I want to let off steam." He pulled her up from the chair and savaged her lips with his own. "This is one of the most devastating nights in my life, and not just because my sister is thirty thousand feet up in the air with some gun-toting madman. And you think I can let off steam by talking?" His hands tore cruelly at her hair. Once again his lips came crashing down on hers.

Eileen wrestled herself free. "How dare you?" she cried.

"Ah, the voice of outraged innocence," Matt snarled. "I thought you liked sex. You little hypocrite."

"You're lower than Keith," Eileen hissed. "He may have wanted to have more than one woman in his life, but he never used one as a substitute for another." She sank back into the leather chair.

"Substitute!" Matt's arms fell to his sides. "Whatever on earth do you mean?"

"I feel genuinely terrible about what you're going through at the moment. But there are limits to the lengths I'm willing to go in order to console you because Helga won't be sharing your bed tonight."

"You fool," Matt got out. "You fool."

"Yes, you've said that to me before. I know you think a woman is very stupid to pass up a chance at a night with you, and maybe you're right. I've no doubt that with all your experience you're an exceedingly accomplished lover. But technical thrills aren't what I'm after. I leave that to the likes of Régine Longemalle."

"Oh, darling." To Eileen's utter disbelief, Matt was suddenly shaking with laughter. "Oh, my darling little fool of a genius. I've never gone to bed with either Régine or Helga. Nor have I ever wanted to."

chapter 21

A STORM OF emotions swept over Eileen and threatened to engulf her. It was as if someone had told her that the earth was square. No: It was as if all her life she'd believed that the world was square and someone had just explained that it was round. Because she had no doubt that Matt was telling the truth.

"I don't understand," she finally managed to say. "All the evidence—"

"Evidence! What evidence!" The tenderness she'd heard in his voice a moment earlier was gone. "You believed what you wanted to believe."

"What I wanted to believe? Are you mad?"

He gripped her shoulders with such force that she cried out. He didn't relax his grip. "You wanted to believe I was like your ex-husband. Like Alan Scott. You wanted to believe I was like them—because you wanted to be able to dismiss me." He shook her. "But you couldn't, could you?" He laughed a laugh both bitter and triumphant. "Because you desired me, didn't you? You desire me still." He lay one hand against the side of her neck; he nodded his satisfaction at the rapidly beating pulse he detected there. Then he dropped his hands to his side. Her body felt bereft of his touch. "That's not good enough," he whispered harshly. "You have to want all of me. More than you want anything else. Even your career."

"My career?" The room seemed to rock and reel around Eileen. "Matt, you've got it all backward. I thought that you were the one who only wanted me for—" She stared

155

at him in bewilderment. She felt as if she were conversing in a language she'd never even heard of before, or dealing with arcane mathematics utterly beyond her scope. "I don't understand," she said simply. "The blue scarf. The way you seemed so— so close to Helga. And then the way Régine clung to you. It was so obvious."

"Obvious, was it?" Matt mocked. "Obvious only because you begin with the preconception that all men are basically playboys. Let me straighten you out a little. Helga and Vee were roommates at flight attendants' school. I've known her nearly half my life. She's been like a second sister to me. I could no more imagine a romantic relationship with her than I could with Vee. The scarf was a present to cheer her up because she's been going through a bad passage with the man who *is* her lover.

Eileen sat silently digesting what Matt had told her. She believed him absolutely, and yet she couldn't make his words mesh with the notions that still had root in her mind. "And Régine?" she asked after a while.

"Come off it," Matt said disgustedly. "At least give me credit for a little taste. Don't you know a game-player when you see one? Régine and Jean-Claude Longemalle keep their marriage going by putting each other down in public— and making up in private. Did you really think that she and I—?" He jammed his hands into his pockets. "I've heard of people looking at the world through rose-colored glasses. You look at men through green-colored glasses. But it's easier that way, isn't it? If you can mentally dismiss men as so many animals, you don't have any troubling romantic feelings coming between you and your Madison Avenue ambitions."

"Talk about misconceptions!" Eileen set her glass down with a thump. "My job has just been a way of paying the bills, that's all. Okay, maybe I got a little bit caught up in the Mont Blanc campaign, but— Matt. I don't understand. Whatever made you think I put my career ahead of everything else?"

He glowered. "It was the kindest construction I could

put on your friendship with Alan Scott. To my mind it would have been an insult to you—an insult I was incapable of—to imagine that you actually liked him. And why," his voice beginning to thunder again, "did you accept that watch from Jean-Claude Longemalle except to cement a business connection?"

"Alan needed my friendship," Eileen burst out. "And maybe I needed to be needed that way instead of just as— you know. As for accepting the watch, I admit: I did worry a little bit that to refuse it would have been to anger *Monsieur* Longemalle and risk losing the account. Losing the account wouldn't have made much difference to my position with Marsden, since I'm just a secretary, but it could have made a lot of difference in Alan's career. I guess the main reason I took it, though, was to get at you and Régine."

To her astonishment, Matt's face lit up. "Truly? You cared that much?"

"Didn't you know?" she asked softly. "I was so sure you knew and just didn't give a damn. Or else were sort of reveling in it because it flattered you. Well, for what it's worth," she finished, "I returned the watch to *Monsieur* Longemalle today. Even though I had still more reason to think that Alan might be in trouble if Longemalle canceled the account." She told Matt about the transatlantic phone call in which Alan had claimed credit for the "Buy Time" slogan.

Matt whistled. "And you said Alan wouldn't hurt you?"

"But don't you see? He hasn't. He can't. Because what happens to me at the Marsden Agency is no big deal one way or the other."

"You mean any job is all right so long as it lets you go on living in New York."

"No, Matt. That's not what I mean at all. I'm not like you. I'm not really happy living just anywhere—or no-where. I've done that since I was a child. I want to put down roots somewhere." She looked sadly around the room. "If I can find welcoming soil."

The tall architect stared at her. "You think I'm unlike

you? It's never occurred to you that a man who builds houses for other people might like to build one for himself, and for his family?"

"But Vee said—" Eileen stopped in midsentence, trying to put yet another piece into the giant jigsaw puzzle she was assembling in her mind.

"Said what?"

"Said that you were always getting mixed up with Ms. Wrong. It just didn't sound like a man who was thinking about home and family."

"That's exactly what I was thinking about. And exactly what the women I kept meeting weren't thinking about. I never made a home for myself because it would only have been a pale shadow, a mockery, of what I really wanted. Of what I still want."

His dark eyes sought her glance and held it. The moment had an enormity that terrified Eileen. It was a giant white-capped wave that she wanted to run headlong into—and that she wanted to run screaming from.

"So many changes," she murmured. "Do I finally know who you are? Do you finally know who I am?"

"I felt I knew you the first moment I saw you," Matt whispered. "It was as if I'd always known you; as if I'd been waiting for you."

"Yes," Eileen echoed. "That was what I felt. Exactly. You were the man I'd dreamed about at seventeen and then gave up believing existed. Now I don't know what to believe."

"When we walked up the Grand'rue together," Matt continued, "when we had breakfast together, every word you said and every move you made confirmed my feeling. Then when you didn't show up at the Chandelier—"

"But I did, Matt. A mere twenty minutes late." Eileen's voice shook. Her stomach churned at the memory of the agony of racing breathlessly to the Old Town only to find that Matt wasn't there.

"Mere twenty minutes! Damn it, lady, I was there half an hour early, I was so eager to be with you again. I didn't want to risk the possibility of missing out on one shared moment. And then when you—" His voice faltered. His eyes narrowed. He drew a deep breath. "It might help you to understand to know that there was a woman in my life. For about a year. A New Yorker. The editor of an architecture magazine. A very sharp business head, she had. Probably never late for an appointment in her life. Only she was always late with me. It drove me wild after a while. It was her way of trying to control me—because I was so controlling. Or so her analyst said."

"Oh," Eileen said, softly. "What— What happened between the two of you, finally?"

"I gave her a very expensive wrist watch. On which I engraved, 'Time wounds all heels.'"

Eileen giggled. "Matt. You didn't."

"Didn't I just?"

"But you—Do you still see her her?" Eileen held her breath.

"I went to see her the last time I was in New York. And her husband—the man who had been her analyst. I came away with the feeling that I had had a very narrow escape. Nice woman, pretty, smart—but as wrong for me as they come. Meeting you was the final confirmation of the rightness of that feeling."

A sweet silence descended on the room. The fire had simmered down to a pile of glowing embers. Eileen thought she saw a hint of gray at the windows facing east. There was so much she wanted to ask Matt, so much she wanted to tell him. But where to begin? Better just to sit back for the moment and drink in the relative peace that hovered between them.

This was not, however, a night for peace—even relative. A wail sounded from the nursery. Eileen and Matt exchanged glances and ran upstairs to find a soaking-wet Marie.

"You change her diaper and pajamas. I'll change the crib," Matt said.

"You know how to do that?" Eileen asked. She lifted

the baby onto the changing table and bent solicitously over her. "Hush, darling. Everything's all right. Matt and Eileen are here."

"Do I know how to change a crib?" Matt retorted, deftly making a bundle of wet sheet, pad, and rubber liner, and replacing them with dry linens. "You know, *Mademoiselle* Connor, you have some screwy notions about men. We'll have to do something about that. Ah, there's a happier looking baby." He plucked Marie from Eileen's arms and held her up over his head. "Hi, pumpkin. All dry, pumpkin?"

Marie started to cry again. "Crib," she sobbed. "Want crib."

"Is that how you're going to change my notions?" Eileen snapped at Matt. "Can't you see that she's too sleepy to play? She just wants to get back to her dreams."

A chagrined look on his face, Matt tenderly arranged Marie in the crib. The baby put two fingers in her mouth, turned onto her side, and fell back asleep at once.

"I'm sorry I snapped at you," Eileen whispered. "I know you meant well."

"That's not always good enough, though, is it?"

Eileen suddenly had the feeling that she couldn't handle one more question, large or small. Vee dominated her thoughts again. She felt tired in every bone. She sank down on the cot. "I think I've got to crash," she said softly. "Do you mind if I desert you?"

"It's probably a good idea. I'll put out the fire, then go to sleep myself." His face grew grim. "Lord knows what we'll have to face tomorrow."

"I'm sorry," Eileen said, "about the crack I made about Helga not— not sharing your bed tonight. It was a terrible cheap shot. I'm so ashamed. I want you to know that I prayed for her safe return, even when I thought you and she—"

"Of course you did, darling. I have a feeling that if we try to apologize to each other for every wrongheaded thing we've thought or said, we'll never get around to discussing anything else." Matt gently ruffled Eileen's feathery hair. "And we do have rather a lot of other things to discuss."

From the other side of the room came the sound of Marie softly moaning in her sleep. Matt crossed to the crib, adjusted a coverlet, then came back to Eileen. "I want to kiss you," he whispered. "Yet somehow I feel I mustn't."

"I know." Eileen looked up at him, let her eyes feast on his pared-down planes, on the vitality that shone through the overlay of worry and weariness. "It's as though we've gone beyond the moment for kisses. From now on it's got to be either more or less."

"You mean," Matt said, "it's got to be everything or nothing."

"Yes, that's it."

He kneeled down on the bed and they clung briefly to each other. Then Matt turned and, without looking back, left the room.

chapter 22

EILEEN SAT BOLT upright in her bed. She opened her eyes. Someone was pounding on the door. The nursery was flooded with daylight. The crib was empty. The little Alpine cottage cuckoo clock over the changing table said ten-twenty. What on earth was happening?

"Eileen!" The door burst open. An exuberant Matt ran in, scooped her up as if she were a child, swung her around, and cried out, "They're safe. They're safe. Vee is safe! They're all safe."

Tears streamed out of Eileen's eyes. "Oh, Matt!" She flung her arms around him and hugged him as hard as she could. "I'm so happy! Now put me down this instant and tell me everything. When will Vee be home? When did the call come? Have you talked to her? Why didn't you wake me? Where's Marie?"

"You're a one-woman press corps," Matt complained affectionately. He set her down on the edge of the bed. "Lord, isn't it marvelous? No, don't put on your robe. Let me stare at those creamy shoulders. This is a day for celebrating everything and everyone."

"I'm not being modest, I'm cold," Eileen laughed. She impishly kissed the tip of Matt's nose. She pulled her robe around her. "Now tell me all the details. Is Vee really, truly okay?"

Vee had sounded absolutely marvelous, Matt assured Eileen. She'd said she was looking forward to a big steak, a nap, a few laps around the pool at a hotel in Bogota, flying an empty plane back to Dakar since Swissair didn't have a Bogota-Dakar run, then working normal Dakar-Geneva service and rejoining the family early Sunday morning.

Eileen was aghast. "You mean she has to *work* after that ordeal?"

"It's like getting right back on a horse after you've been thrown. She said she was looking forward to the run, that incredible sister of mine. You know what she said the worst part of the hijacking was? Next to having to worry about all of us going crazy with worry back here? The boredom! That blasted gunman wouldn't let the crew converse except about technical essentials because he was afraid they'd talk in code and plot against him. Can you imagine Vee having to endure an overseas flight without a good gossip?"

"Oh, God." Eileen clapped her hands in the manner of an excited little girl. "It's so marvelous that she's safe. But who—?"

They were interrupted by the sudden appearance of a transformed Coco, her cookie face decorated with beaming smile and happy eyes. She held a laden tray in her hands. It was an absolute disgrace, she chided Matt, that he was talking Eileen's ear off without Eileen having had so much as a sip of coffee. Matt took the tray from her hands and set it down at bedside.

"Coco, you angel," Eileen exclaimed. "I'm desperate for coffee. And don't tell me you baked those *croissants* yourself!"

"And who else if not me? I got up with the crows this morning, and it was a choice of baking something very complicated or going mad with worry about our darling Vee. Then of course we got the grand news, and a good thing it was that I'd done the baking, because the appetites around here since the phone call have been quite something." Coco flashed one last beaming smile on Matt and Eileen, then claimed a pressing task in the kitchen and left them on their own.

As Matt poured coffee and steamed milk into two large

mugs, Eileen leaned back against a heap of flower-patterned pillows and mentally framed the moment. The sunlight in the darling little nursery, the casual masculine grace with which Matt presided over his small task, the warmth and sparkle left behind by Coco, and above all the stupendous news from Bogota! The moment was one she wanted to be able to file in her mind and glance upon at will. She didn't know what would become of her and Matt. The terrible tension between them was gone. They'd erased some misunderstandings. Yet so much remained to be resolved . . . if indeed it could be resolved. All the more reason to venerate this moment.

"I think Coco suspects something," Eileen murmured, then instantly regretted the words as her damnable blush did its usual work on her cheeks.

"Suspects something? Hopes something is more like it," Matt said. "Coco has seen it all." He traced an imaginary outline around the rash of red on her cheeks. "Well?"

"Well what?"

"We're not going to disappoint her, are we?"

"Oh, Matt. You can probably think of more excuses for making love than a cat can think of for drinking cream." Eileen tried to sound disapproving, but she ended up laughing. She felt so high—high on the news about Vee's safety, high on the gorgeous morning, high on the presence of Matt. "Don't you want your coffee?" she tried.

"Afterward," Matt said. He gave Eileen a look so intense that she knew the time had come. "You know that I—"

"Shh," she said. Suddenly she felt the same surge of confidence, the same certainty that she could not betray herself, that she'd had during their very first encounter in the dress shop in the Old Town. "No more words. We've had too many words. We've all but done ourselves in with words."

She shrugged off the robe that she'd drawn about her shoulders moments before. Matt moved toward her, but she held up a cautionary hand. She wanted him to know that the games were over, the chase was ended. He wasn't taking her; she was giving herself. Her hands went to the spaghetti straps of her nightgown and untied the two bows. She sat up proudly as the bodice of her nightgown fell away, revealing her breasts.

Matt's eyes, his hands, his lips paid homage to her beauty. Then the two of them were stretched out together on the narrow bed, tugging at each other's clothes, tearing away the last remaining barriers between them, bonding the molecules of their separate bodies and beings. Suddenly it no longer mattered to Eileen who was giving and who was taking; she and Matt were one. And she knew that although she had surrendered her virginity to her ex-husband, Keith, Matt was the first man to whom she had truly surrendered herself.

Afterward, as she lay in his arms, she said softly, "So that's what it's all about."

He tightened his hold on her. "Just the beginning, my darling."

"You mean that wasn't—enough for you?"

"Oh," Matt said soberly, "it was everything. But with you I'll always want more than everything."

"Greedy," she chided affectionately, as his hands made themselves known to every inch of her skin.

"Aren't I just? But greedy on your behalf, too. I want you to feel sensations you didn't even know were there to be felt. I want everything to happen between us, Eileen; the whole panoply of human experiences."

"Does it all have to happen before lunch?"

"Oh, you wag," Matt laughed. "How mercilessly you mock me. No, I'd say we have time. All the time in Switzerland—and everywhere else, too."

"That's good to hear. Because right now I'm desperate for coffee," Eileen said.

"Whatever my darling desires." Matt helped her slip into her robe, shrugged on his own clothes, then handed her a mug of *café au lait*. "It's probably too cool now."

"I could do with a bit of coolness. No," as she sipped, "it's just right." She looked at Matt. "Everything in the whole world is just right. Now tell me how I slept through all the commotion this morning. Where's Marie?"

"Pierre woke up needing those sticky little hugs and kisses. So he tiptoed in and stole her away."

"Wasn't it amazing how she picked up on our anxiety last night? Children have incredible antennas." She reached over and broke off a bit of the buttery, flaky *croissant* Coco had baked. "Matt. I still don't know how the hijacking happened. Who was the gunman? How did he carry the operation off? How did it all end?"

"Vee was only allowed to give us a sketchy outline. There's going to be a debriefing for the crew, and an investigation by the airline and other aviation authorities, and until it's over the crew has been cautioned not to compromise security." He grimaced. "Now they worry about security! If that isn't the original case of locking the barn door after the horse escaped, I don't know what is."

"Well, tell me what you do know."

One of the passengers on the Hong Kong flight, Matt reported, was a man who normally worked as a baggage handler at the Geneva airport, known to the flight crew; and everyone working aboard the aircraft made a point of being friendly and accommodating. Several hours after takeoff, a junior hostess—not Vee or Helga—let him accompany her into the first-class galley because he claimed to be deeply curious about in-flight food preparation, and there he pulled a gun on her and demanded that she take him into the cockpit.

"How did he get a gun past the metal detectors?" Eileen asked.

"That's one of the questions the investigation hopes to answer. He may not have gone through one of the normal passenger checkpoints, even though he was on vacation and in civilian dress. He could have used his ID card to get into the restricted area and then just have proceeded like any other passenger. We'll know eventually, I guess."

Eileen shuddered. "Do they know why he did it? Was it a grievance against the airline or something?"

"It seems he had a brother who was serving a heavy term in jail in Bogota after a big cocaine-ring bust. He thought he could persuade the Colombian authorities to release his brother in exchange for the lives of the flight crew. The authorities tricked him into letting a couple of supercops on board, and that was that. No shots fired. Now the wretched devil can join his brother—in jail."

Matt and Eileen looked at each other. The hijacking drama and all its possible ramifications hung in the air between them. Eileen tried to comprehend the sick mind that had perpetrated the event. The effort made her faintly dizzy. The pristine brightness of the day suddenly looked smudged and stained.

"It's hard to believe that life just goes on after such a thing. And yet there's Vee, thinking about a steak and a swim, as though nothing had happened. The human psyche is an extraordinary thing." She absently fingered the satin edge of the blanket on her bed. "It makes you ashamed of all the times you've collapsed over some trifle, doesn't it?"

Matt's face went sober. "I'm afraid there's a rather pre- dictable syndrome following an event like a hijacking. We've already had a call from one of the medical personnel with the airline. First there's a period of euphoria—that's what Vee and Helga are feeling right now. Then later, apparently, there are often nightmares and bouts of depres- sion and sometimes an inability to work. In fact, once they've done their getting-back-on-the-horse routine, the members of Vee's crew will be permitted to take as much time off as they feel they need. And if they want counseling of any sort, it will be available to them."

"Oh." Eileen's voice was small. Then, "I don't know Helga, but Vee seems to be one of the strongest people I've ever met. If she could survive what happened to your par- ents, she can probably survive anything. And she has so much to fall back on. You and Marie and Pierre, and this wonderful house, and Coco; and, well, there aren't any real money pressures, are there? So if she wanted to stop work- ing for a while she could."

"You know how she loves her work. She may be happiest when she's home with her baby and her husband, but she needs the socialness of flying. I agree with you, though. If anyone can get through a crisis like this without being scarred, it's Vee. Actually, Helga's the one I'm more worried about."

Eileen looked down. She hated herself for being jealous, but jealous she was—despite what Matt had said about his relationship with Helga, despite the simple inappropriateness of jealousy at such a moment.

Looking down didn't hide her emotions from Matt. She felt his large hand cupping her small chin. He forced her to face him, to meet his eyes. "Let me tell you about Helga," he said. His voice was neutral. "Let me tell you about my good buddy Helga, my second sister. She's in love with a pilot. She's been in love with him for years. He's married. He won't get a divorce. No, my moppet, I can see what you're thinking. Don't be so quick to judge. Flashy blond husband-stealer, right? Another one of those fly-by-night flygirls? It's not exactly the case here. The pilot is a pretty straight-up guy. He's absolutely mad about Helga. He's also a gentleman—too much of a gentleman, if you ask me. He won't sue his wife for divorce even though she's taken considerable advantage of his absences from home, if you get my meaning; even though she's made it clear that the main reason she hasn't left *him* is that she doesn't want to give up the status and free flights that go along with being Mrs. Pilot."

"Are there children?" Eileen asked.

"Are you kidding? Mrs. Pilot is too selfish and narcissistic to have kids. That's another tragic aspect to the story, another reason I'm plenty worried about what Helga will have to fall back on. The pilot wants kids. She wants kids. And she's forty. She can't wait a whole lot longer. I have a feeling that this brush with mortal danger is going to make her even more desperately eager to be a mama."

Eileen tried to smile. "I want to like her. I do feel sorry for her, from what you say. I'm sure if you and Vee and Pierre like her, she's a fine person. But—" The image of a blue chiffon scarf floated into her mind once again.

"Matt," she whispered. "I still have trouble getting everything in order in my mind. So many notions to overturn."

He stood up. "Do you doubt my word?" he asked harshly. "Do you still believe that Helga and I—"

"No," she said urgently. "And yet, I have to admit I'm still jealous. I hate the jealousy, but—" She shrugged. She nibbled on a thumbnail. "It's just there. I don't know how to make it go away."

"I wonder," Matt said meditatively. "Don't you—" He was interrupted by a small redheaded bombshell hurling herself into his arms.

"Walk!" Marie cried. She pointed to the window and the world beyond. "Marie want walk!"

"Where's your papa?"

"Papa shower. Walk!"

Matt smiled at Eileen. "I seem to have my marching orders. I suspect this discussion has gone as far as it can go at the moment, anyway. Do you mind if I take the sprout out?"

"Of course not. I want to wash and dress. It's almost noon. What a lazy old thing I am."

"Shall we wait for you? We have a favorite walk up into the woods. I'm sure Marie would like to show it to you."

"No, you go ahead. Marie, darling, come give Eileen a kiss. I love you, baby."

"I hope you can someday see your way clear to directing those words my way," Matt said, a faint trace of mockery in his voice.

"I hope I can," Eileen answered, not mockingly at all.

chapter 23

DEAR TALL STRANGER

I am leaving this note with Coco because I must, simply must, go back to Geneva and be by myself to sort out the events of the last twenty-four hours. Perhaps it's cowardly of me to run off like this. (There's a 1:15 train I hope to make.) But I feel as though we've gotten to the point of no-return. I mean: It's no longer a question of you understanding me and me understanding you as much as it's a question of you understanding you and me understanding me. It's as though the last barriers to happiness lie within each of us, not between us.

Please explain what happened to Pierre, and tell Marie that I'll see her soon.

Matt: I wrote to the tall stranger once before. Maybe someday I'll show you that letter.

Why is there still a murkiness? When everything in a way is crystal clear?

A thought comes to me. *Little One and the Tall Stranger* was a glorious drama in its way. Full of pitfalls, also full of splendid excitement. But maybe it has to be laid to rest. If we are to go any further.

Extraordinary how right we've been about each other, and how wrong!

Darling. I write "darling" with a firm hand, and yet there is a part of me that dreads the possibility I may once again have misunderstood you, that I'm assuming feelings on your part I shouldn't be assuming.

For God's sake, Matt: If that is the case, let me know at once. Cut me free.

It's been the most extraordinary day in my life in the most extraordinary week in my life. Going from the depths of misery because of Vee, soaring to the heights of happiness as we finally revealed ourselves to each other.

Yet feeling: We can go higher still. We have to, or we might as well turn our backs on each other.

I have to go now. I guess that's all there is to say for the moment anyway.

—Eileen

chapter 24

AS THE TRAIN pulled out of Vevey and started toward Geneva, Eileen was suddenly breathless at her own boldness. Never in her life, not even when she was married, had she so opened herself to a man—and let him see that openness.

Half of her wished she could go back to the Lenkes' house and rip up the note she'd left with the understanding Coco. The other half knew she'd made the only possible move. The time for game-playing, for cowering behind illusions, was over.

As she watched the brilliant blue of Lake Geneva flash by, she thought: That's how everything should be between men and women. Clear as the Lake. Even though clarity can be so frightening.

Eileen walked the few blocks from the train station to her hotel. She realized that she no longer had to look at street signs. She instinctively knew when to turn. I'm going to miss this city, she thought. She longed to slip into a dream about a future which entailed frequent visits to Geneva, but she forebade herself the escape.

No dreams. Dreams were illusions, too.

At the hotel she found a pile of messages from Alan and Samantha. The most recent one read: "Just heard the great news over the radio. So happy. We've gone for a hike up Le Salève. Back around six. Drinks???? Love, A & S."

Eileen grinned all the way up to her room. Only a few days earlier, Alan had said that hiking up Le Salève wasn't at all his idea of fun. Apparently Samantha had persuaded him to see things differently. Then Eileen's grin faded. Was the hike really such a good sign, after all? It was one thing to be adventurous, to try things. But one had to be true to oneself. A romance built on any other foundation was built on sand.

Could she and Matt be true to themselves and true to each other? That was the question, wasn't it?

She let herself into her room. She looked around. It felt somehow different. Then she realized: The flowers that Jean-Claude Longemalle had sent her were gone. The last few blooms must have withered and the maid taken the arrangement away. Eileen felt a small pang. It was as if summer had ended before she was quite ready for fall.

Eileen began unpacking the small bag she had taken to Vevey. A knock sounded at the door. She opened it. A chambermaid who couldn't have been more than eighteen was standing there, shyly holding the ceramic fondue dish that had held Monsieur Longemalle's original arrangement. Springing up out of it were a few yellow daisies.

"I hope *madame* does not mind," the maid began, "that I took the liberty of changing the water and rearranging the survivors."

Eileen wanted to hug her. "They look beautiful," she said warmly. "Thank you."

She took the few flowers and put them on her dresser. They seemed a living symbol of hope. It struck her at that moment how much she was hoping for.

She started a bath. She pulled off her crimson velvet jeans. They were ready for another trip to the cleaner's. Eileen made a face at the thought of a day without them. They were so comfortable. She felt so much herself in them. "And yet," she said aloud, "without Matt, you never would have bought them. Sometimes change is a move toward truth, not away from it. When you were wearing the clothes you picked out, my dear Eileen, you weren't really being true to yourself. Not to your best self, anyway. Just to some scared self. A sort of anti-Eileen."

She would go back to the boutique called Une Vie Nouvelle, she decided abruptly, and buy another pair of jeans.

A couple more tops. Maybe another dress. She let the water out of the tub and got the shower running. She was too impatient for a bath. Yes: Whatever the future held for her, she would face it in red. The days of gray were over. For good. Not just because Matt wanted her in red. Because she wanted herself in red.

For one last time, she put on a skirt and sweater the color of smoke. A plan was forming in her mind, and if she could put it into action, she wouldn't need any more office clothes. She would leave the whole lot behind in Geneva and ask Vee to give them to a charity thrift shop.

Once again she crossed the Mont Blanc bridge. Once again she was a woman with a purpose, hurrying past swans and Flower Clock, promising herself to dawdle and admire later. Once again she angled up the Grand'Rue. Once again the dimensions and twists of the street cast a spell on her and made her feel that anything might happen.

She walked into the small, jazzy shop. Instinctively she looked toward the counter where she'd first seen the tall stranger, first seen Matt Edwards. His absence was almost as palpable this day as his presence had been stunning that other day. Her eye fell on the box of silk scarves he'd been going through when she got that initial heart-stopping glimpse of him. It sat neglected-looking next to a box of leather gloves.

"Ah, *madame*. Welcome back." Eileen looked up to see the clerk who'd helped her during her spree of buying red.

"I've enjoyed what I bought here so much," Eileen told the clerk. "I want more. More jeans, another sweater, maybe a casual skirt." She took out a folder of travelers' checks. "I have a few hundred dollars. I want to leave it all behind in this shop."

"An agreeable and simple task," the clerk smiled. She stared at Eileen, then nodded. "I thought something had changed in *madame*. You have had your hair cut. Most becoming."

Forty-five minutes later, Eileen had a new wardrobe. As she looked at the array of reds and pinks spread out beside

the cash register, she mentally flashed to Matt's latest painting, the explosion of circles, the study in scarlet. Not that
the clothes could remotely hold a candle to the brillance of
his work; still, the connection felt valid in her mind.

Everything was starting to connect now. Slowly, everything was starting to connect, the puzzle filling in.

As Eileen walked back to the Hotel Richemond, she felt
overwhelmed by a sense of peace. Uncertainties still existed.
In a sense, they still abounded. But a feeling prevailed that
she could not err now, could not betray herself or anyone
else. She was centered. That was it. Very close, anyway.

"Your compass is set at true north." In her mind she
heard Matt speaking those words at the Longemalle's party,
as they embraced during that exquisite moment-out-of-con-
text when the lights were extinguished—and the rules of the
game were suspended. "Your compass is set at true north.
But then there's that whole other layer in the way. All your
notions. Trust yourself. Trust me."

She'd flinched at those words. They'd seemed part of
a come-on. They'd reminded her all too sharply of the time
when the treacherous Keith had asked for her trust. Now,
as she listened to Matt's gravelly voice echo in her mind,
the words were a beacon of light.

Trusting herself and trusting Matt weren't two different
acts, two different conditions; they were one gorgeous in-
tertwined state of being.

"Yes," she proclaimed to the Lake, as she crossed the
Mont Blanc bridge toward the Right Bank; "I can begin to
trust Matt because I can begin to trust my own judgment.
And in part I trust my own judgment because it's wise
enough to trust him."

She paused to look at an eight- or nine-year-old girl and
her younger brother. They were leaning off the bridge,
throwing bread to the swans. The swans ignored them, to
the great frustration of the children. Immediately a story
began to form in Eileen's mind, a story about a swan who
only ate bread from a certain bakery. It might be an amusing
parable for parents to read to kids who were fussy eaters.

A refrain came to mind. "There's only one crust I trust."

Suddenly she threw back her head and roared with laughter. The two children with the bread turned to look at her. How could she possibly explain the thought that had just come to her? There's only one crust I trust. Matt Edwards. She gave the children what she hoped was a reassuring smile and continued on.

As the crossed the lobby of the Richemond, she steeled herself for the possibility that there would be no message from Matt. That he would call sooner or later was a certainty. He had to know that she awaited a response to her note with trembling eagerness. He would call, if only to tell her that he could not make the final leap to her side. But *when* he would call was another matter. He would not want to act precipitously. She might not hear from him for days.

Still the desk clerk's negative response to her inquiry was a blow. The openness she'd experienced on her walk home threatened to desert her. It took all her will to turn her mind from thoughts of Matt. She would go upstairs, she decided, change into one of her new outfits, sit down at her desk, and write out the story of the fussy swan. She would not simply tread water. She would not pace.

Fifteen minutes later, clad in a red and white checked shirt with rolled-up sleeves and a pair of pink corduroy jeans, she was deep into the story. The swan's name was Billy, and he swam faster than all the other swans on Lake Geneva, and everyone like him very much, and the one problem he had in the world was that he only liked the bread from Madame Tour's Bake Shop, and—

And the telephone rang.

Matt. Matt reaching for her across the miles and calling her his dearest darling and saying he understood her leaving and her note was an act of great courage and they were almost there, they were almost there.

"I have an idea," he said.

"Tell me. Anything."

"It was your idea, actually. About putting little one and the tall stranger to rest. I think— Well, let's go back to the place where we both took a wrong turn. The first of all those wrong turns. Let's exorcise the last ghost between us. Meet me at the Chandelier tonight. At eight."

She gasped. "It feels like tempting fate," she whispered.

"That's exactly why we're doing it. We're going to tempt fate, and fate is not going to trip us up."

"I guess we really have to, don't we?"

"I think we do."

For a moment there was silence. She felt his fingers gripping her shoulders, his lips pressing into her lips. She leaned into the sensation, she lost herself in it.

Then his voice was saying, smiling and yet not smiling, "I'll see you tonight. Don't be late."

chapter **25**

SHE WAS LATE.

The late Eileen Connor, mentally kicking and screaming at this cruel trick of the gods, happened to be a passenger on the first elevator to get stuck in the entire history of the internationally renowned Hotel Richemond.

The irony within the irony of the event was that if she hadn't been so eager, so determined, to be at the Chandelier five minutes early, she wouldn't have stepped into the ill-fated elevator when she did. She would have been sauntering over to the doorman, requesting a taxi, at seven-forty-five instead of dashing, nauseated, to a phone booth at eight-eighteen.

She put money in the phone. She dailed. She prayed.

"*Bon soir. Le Chandelier*," a woman's voice lilted.

"*Monsieur* Matt Edwards. In the bar. Please. Please."

"I'll see if he's here, *madame*."

A kaleidescope of thoughts whirled through Eileen's mind. Memories of standing in a phone booth trying to get through to Vevey after hearing about the hijacking. Pictures of Marie and her toy kangaroo. Billy the swan singing, "I only trust one crust." Matt holding her. Matt kissing her. Matt shouting at her. Matt laughing at her.

Matt leaving the Chandelier Monday night because she was a few minutes late.

Matt—

And then real and actual Matt Edwards was on the phone, was all concern and affection, was saying: "Darling? Are you all right? Are you all right, Eileen?"

178

She closed her eyes to hold back the tears of pure relief. "You're there," was all she could say. "You waited."

"Of course I waited. But it was so dreadful. I knew how much you'd want to be on time tonight. And as the minutes passed, my imagination produced the most horrifying thoughts. What on earth happened? Are you all right?"

"A stuck elevator. I'm fine. Everyone is fine. It was merely one of the worst half-hours of my life. But I'm fine. I'm going to walk, darling. I need the air. I'll be there in ten or fifteen minutes, okay?"

"Take your time. I'll be here."

All the way to the Old Town she replayed his last words on her mental phonograph. "Take your time. I'll be here." They buoyed her. They warmed her. They washed away the terrible half-hour when she was locked between two floors at the hotel, wondering if her chance at happiness was over.

Matt stood to greet her when she walked into the bar at the Chandelier. It was as if the sun were rising just to light her day.

"Hello, Eileen." He bestowed a whispery soft kiss on her mouth. In its own way that kiss stung more than the fiercest embrace they had shared.

"Hello, Matt."

"Do you want to move to a table?"

"No, I like it here at the bar." She did like it, the bustling, peopled warmth of the place, the rows of bottles reflected in the mirror behind them, the cheerful presence of the bartender. And she wanted to wallow in the contrast between this night and that other night, that most dreadful night of waiting.

"I've been drinking white wine," Matt said, "but I thought I'd switch to champagne, if that's all right with you."

"Sure it is."

"Not just to celebrate us, though Lord knows that would be reason enough." He tenderly traced an imaginary line down one of her rosy cheeks.

"You mean to celebrate the fantastic news from Bogota."

"And yet more," Matt said. He looked at her. "Helga. Her great love, the pilot, called us after you left the house. He said he wanted us to know that the hijacking was a kind of apocalypse for him. It made him realize, once and forever, that there could be no happiness for him without Helga. So he offered his wife a choice. She could divorce him, or he would divorce her."

"Oh, Matt!" Eileen's face radiated pleasure. "That's just so marvelous! I'm thrilled."

"You are, by God, aren't you! Rather a change, I would say."

"A change?" A sudden awareness jolted Eileen. "It is a change, isn't it? You're so right. I don't see Helga as the enemy anymore. No more jealousy." She looked down at her hands as though unable to believe they were empty. "No more jealousy at all. It's just gone."

The bartender produced a silver bucket of ice out of which blossomed, like some splendid organic thing, a green bottle with a mushroom-shaped cork. He held the bottle up so Matt could inspect the label.

"Perfect," Matt said.

The bartender popped the cork and poured a small amount of the bubbling wine into a glass. Matt tasted it and nodded. The bartender filled Eileen's glass, then Matt's. He smiled his satisfaction with the moment, then left Matt and Eileen on their own.

Matt raised his glass. "Shall we drink to all our happy landings?"

Eileen raised her glass. "I'll drink to that."

They sipped. Eileen sighed. "How will I ever go back to Coca-Cola?" She sighed humorously.

"You don't have to, you know," Matt said. Once again his voice had the offhand tone that, ironically, seemed to accompany his most loaded statements. "I'd very much like the honor of keeping you in champagne."

Eileen's cheeks flamed so hotly that her ears felt singed. "Matt—"

He held up his hand. "Wait. There have been too many misunderstandings between us. I'm not taking any chances. This is no moment for metaphors. I'm asking you to be my wife. I love you, Eileen. Will you marry me?"

Eileen looked at the dark intelligent eyes, the intense contours of the face that had dominated her dreams for so long. Her body tingled exquisitely. Every step she'd taken in her life had led to this moment, she thought with a profound sense of joy. Every corner she ever turned, every hope she ever had brought her here.

"I never really had a home," she said, when she could trust herself to speak. "I look at you and I think: This is home. My heart's home. My body's home. My soul's home. My mind's home."

"My sweet poet," he murmured, grazing her lips with his. "Are you saying yes to me? Tell me you're saying yes, and make me the happiest man on earth."

"I feel," she said, "as though we've kicked down virtually every barrier between us. Tonight when I was late and you didn't lose faith . . . and then when you talked about Helga and I felt only warmth—"

"What remains?" Matt asked frantically. "Tell me, darling."

"I want you to keep me in champagne. I do. But I want to keep you in champagne, too. Do you understand, Matt? I have to go on working. I can't be the wife I want to be to you if I'm only your wife."

"You call that a barrier? By all means go on working. I can live in New York if I'm with you."

"No, no," she said, laughing. "I don't want to go on working in advertising. I'm finished with Madison Avenue. I had my moment of glory, and now I can leave because even that moment turned out to be hollow. No, what I want to do is write children's books. Marie loved that story of mine, and today I started work on another, and I have a feeling they'll just keep coming. And if we have children, that will only inspire me the more, don't you think? You do want to have children, don't you, Matt?"

"Do you think I practiced changing cribs just for the fun of it?" he thundered. "You knew that night when we took care of Marie that I wanted to have children, didn't you? Wanted to have them with you?"

"I didn't dare think it," Eileen whispered. "It was merely everything I wanted to think." The moment threatened to overwhelm her. She turned to a slightly less emotional topic. "Do you like the idea of the children's books? I could work on them anywhere. We don't have to be in New York at all. Anywhere—as long as you're there. Where are you going?" she asked, as he stood up. "I say yes to you and you run away, is that it?"

His laughter chimed in with hers. "Oh, my darling. Darlingest darling. I'm going to the checkroom. I have something to show you."

A moment later he reappeared carrying a black leather portfolio. "Do you remember the other night at Vevey when Vee mentioned some drawings I'd done for Marie?"

"Yes, of course."

"I brought them. Here. I want you to look at them. I don't mean to impose myself on your art, but if you think any of them might be suitable as illustrations for your books— What's the matter? You look pale. Don't you like that one?"

Eileen was staring at a picture of a swan, a disdainful little swan with a turned-up bill. "I don't believe it," she gasped. "It's unreal. That's Billy."

"It is, is it? Should I know more about this Billy? A rival for my affections?"

She marveled at the drawing of the swan, then looked in awe and pleasure at the other drawings in the portfolio. Finally she came to something very different. "What's this?" she asked.

"That's a blueprint," Matt said. "My dream house. The one I didn't dare think about building because I didn't dare believe I would find the woman to share it."

Eileen's hand crept into his. She could barely speak. "It's got everything," she finally said. "Master bedroom with a balcony, nursery, and— two studios, Matt?"

"Two. Why not? As long as I was dreaming an impossible dream, I figured I might as well throw in a creative wife. I mean, it was only a dream." He smiled his tenderness, his sense of celebration. "By the way," he added, in his casual voice, "there's some land available halfway between Vevey and Geneva. With a view of the Lake. Does that sound interesting at all to you?"

"Matt Edwards, if you don't stop being so perfect, I'll— I'll—" Eileen spluttered.

"You'll what?"

"I love you so much. Oh, I love you just so much. I'll kiss you passionately, is what I'll do. Even though a tall stranger once told me such things aren't done in public in Geneva."

"Forget about the tall stranger. Forget about everyone but me."

She did.

Introducing a unique new concept in romance novels!
Every woman deserves a…

Second Chance at Love ™

You'll revel in the settings, you'll delight in the
heroines, you may even fall in love with the
magnetic men you meet in the pages of…

Second Chance at Love

Look for three new
novels of lovers lost and found coming ™ every
month from Jove! Available now: